EYES TO DECEIT

EYES TO DECEIT

THE COMPANY FILES: 4

GABRIEL VALJAN

"It may be dangerous to be America's enemy, but to be America's friend is fatal."

"America has no permanent friends or enemies, only interests."

— HENRY KISSINGER

Chapter One

The postcard from Independence, Missouri, arrived, its message handwritten:

'The door is open for your arrival on Wednesday, July 15, between two and four in the afternoon.'

Within the parenthesis of time it took him to drive eighteen hours from Manhattan to Missouri, he stopped once to change clothes, grab a bite, and shave in the restroom of a Howard Johnson.

The dashes of white on the endless blacktop became as rhythmic as a heartbeat. He was driving into the past, into the Middle America of his youth—before Uncle Sam put him in uniform, before he joined the Company.

Walker kept going until he reached North Delaware Street. Slowing down, he read house numbers. His destination was a white Victorian with a metal fence out front. When he spotted it, he parked his Buick behind a Chrysler New Yorker.

He climbed the four steps and found the door ajar, just as the postcard had promised. A melancholic piano melody greeted him. He found the room and stood in the doorway.

A warm breeze stirred a curtain.

His host wore a pressed white shirt and dark slacks. Walker noted the mirror shine on the man's shoes—a habit they both carried over from the military. One foot worked the sustain pedal, the part musicians called the soul of the piano. Manicured fingertips coaxed a delicate theme of memory from the keys.

The pianist, hearing the shift in the room, knew he was no longer alone.

He said, "Recognize the piece?"

"Chopin."

"You have a good ear, friend. Op. 69, No. 1. I played this waltz for Stalin in Potsdam."

"How did it go over?"

"Stalin loved it. Churchill did not."

Walker's lips lifted into a smile. "I imagine Churchill preferred something with cannons."

The music reminded Walker of rain, of mornings in bed with Leslie.

"Introspective, isn't it? The piece reminds me of a fork in the road of life—a decision to be made," the man said. "When I was a young man, I said I'd either play piano in a whorehouse like Brahms, or I'd become a politician. What did I do? I became president of the United States—so you could say I've done both. How was the drive?"

Without seeing the face, Walker sensed a smile. "I made good time, sir."

"I'd like to keep playing, so don't be offended if I keep my back to you."

"You play, I'll listen."

"I read your play on the Rosenbergs. Know what I did the night they were executed?"

A light trill from the keyboard provided contrast to the dark history.

"Bess and I lit out east. We took that Chrysler parked outside, stopped at diners, took in a couple Broadway plays. No Secret Service. We thought of ourselves as John and Jane Doe." The music turned somber. "Gutsy of you to work in old man Kennedy and the daughter's lobotomy."

Walker said, "His son was in the audience. I needed to put a point across. I take it you didn't approve."

The voice said, "Didn't say that. Robert Kennedy did hitch his wagon to McCarthy. You exercised an author's prerogative. The material writes itself. Let's hope Mr. Kennedy sees that for what it was. As for his old man, we clashed. FDR was right to demand his resignation."

It was before the war when Joseph Kennedy resigned his post as ambassador to Great Britain—over policy, and over Hitler.

"Son of a bitch gave the Kremlin all the ammunition it needed. As for

McCarthy, he's not the first demagogue this country's known. Coughlin, Huey Long. People like to say I raised hell, but I told the truth—and they thought it was hell. Listen to this section—right here."

He played *L'Adieu*, published twenty years after Chopin's death. The voice talked over the notes.

"In this section, Chopin says goodbye to love and life. As we all must. We live lives of fateful decisions and consequences. Speaking of which—did you know I was nearly court-martialed? September 1918. I disobeyed a direct order. Familiar with it?"

"I've heard of it. You made the right decision. Saved lives."

The notes faltered—slightly. Fingers remembering risk.

"Or I was just lucky it didn't bite me in the ass." The music dropped out. The voice hardened. "I didn't lose a single man that day, but I disobeyed an order. If Pershing hadn't gone to bat for me, I'd have faced a worse fate than MacArthur."

Walker caught the edge in his tone. And now, for the first time, he saw the man.

"That brings me to why I summoned you."

"Sir?"

"To follow an order—or not. To take the unpleasant path for the greater good."

"Like your decision in September. Or August, with the bomb?"

"The bomb wasn't the hardest choice I made. No—Korea was harder. With Korea, I stopped being the modest man from Missouri. I became Caesar at the Rubicon. History will judge me. I just hope Clio waits until I'm dead before she renders her verdict."

The piano quieted. The former president removed his hands from the keys.

"You, Walker, are at your crossroads. You can't stay innocent."

"I wouldn't call myself innocent, sir."

"I don't mean it as an insult. But let's look at the facts. You joined the Company because Jack Marshall asked you. True?"

"True."

"And you said yes because you didn't know what else to do? Be honest."

"Yes."

"Jack gave you purpose."

Walker remembered a night in Vienna—Leslie had said the same.

Truman turned, swung his legs around. "I knew I was a musician from a young age. You—you took the long road before you realized that you were a writer."

Walker smiled. "Takes some of us longer."

"Ah, the luxury of time and youth."

He gestured toward a chair. Truman chose another. It felt avuncular. Sincere.

Harry S. Truman had always presented himself as a practical man of the people. Homespun, some said. But few understood that farm life meant living with failure, with rot and rain, and quiet violence. Farmers knew the weight of spoiled crops and the sharp truth of an ax in wood.

"I wrote the order that created the Company," Truman said. "I'm also the only president who saw combat abroad. When I conjured it into being, I expected its directors to understand what it meant to take a life. I didn't expect to see the day the Agency would be run by a man who reads names like numbers."

"You dislike Dulles?"

Truman sighed. "Eisenhower's the president. He may not have seen combat, but he bore the agony of command. He sent boys into hell. He gets it. But I'm concerned."

"With Dulles?"

"With Dulles—or the devil himself."

Truman leaned forward, tapped Walker's knee. "You've seen combat. You've seen death. And now you've got a choice."

Walker's throat tightened. "Stay with the Company or leave?"

"Exactly."

"But not both?"

"You tell me. How's it been, doing both?"

"Fiction is truth. Truth, fiction."

Truman nodded. "And the politician says: the lie is truth, the truth a lie."

"A question," Walker said. "Is this about me and the Company, or you and Dulles?"

"I had no choice. I stepped in because the man in the chair before me worked himself to death."

"And now you think something wicked this way comes?"

"I fear Macbeth may be your muse, Walker."

"Strange to think that for the years FDR was president, I met the man twice."

"And your impression?"

Chapter Two

On the interstate into New York City, Walker glanced in the rearview mirror and spotted a police car behind him. He hadn't kept the needle at 65, as that would look too careful, nor had he pushed it past 70, which risked a ticket. Still, the attention puzzled him.

He checked the seat beside him. Nothing but a half-eaten sandwich in crumpled wax paper and a Thermos. One sniff would reveal the only kick in it was caffeine. His .45 was locked in the trunk, paperwork in order. He kept driving, unconvinced at first that the white car was tailing him.

The drive had been an uneventful, miles of flat road, long stretches of nothing, but now he was Ahab, the cruiser behind him his white whale. When the red gumball light flicked on, he eased his Roadmaster onto the shoulder.

No officer approached. That was odd. He knew the routine: one man radios in the stop while the other takes the slow walk up to the window. But the two inside the cruiser did nothing. He waited, falling back on his army training of Sit-and-Wait.

Two minutes later, a Nash Metropolitan rolled into view and idled on the roadside.

It stopped. The police pulled away.

Walker watched the Metro's door swing open and clap shut. A man in a black suit stepped out. The look was corporate—General Motors corporate. Everything about him suggested Howard Roark, except this man hadn't leapt from the pages of *The Fountainhead*. He was a Company man. Walker thought he recognized him.

The man approached with a bureaucrat's posture of shoulders squared, expression scrubbed of anything human. He stood at the door. Silent.

Walker looked in the direction of the departed law enforcement vehicle. "What's with roping in the locals?" Nothing. Walker looked in his rearview mirror at the man's partner in the vehicle. "Isn't your buddy joining us?"

"Why should he?"

"What's with the stop?"

The fictional Howard said, "A change of plans."

"When and where?"

"When is today, and the where is 630 Fifth Avenue."

Walker couldn't suppress the comedian's double-take. "Rockefeller Center?"

"Room 3603, to be more precise."

The messenger stood there, emotionless, his eyes hidden behind sunglasses.

Walker let the words hang in the air before he said, "I'll play the owl and say, Who?"

"The director. He'd like a word with you."

"The director?"

"The Old Man himself."

"Ain't it my lucky day."

"I don't envy you."

Walker held the man's stare for a moment longer than politeness required. "I'll tell him you said hello."

* * *

On the road to the Empire State, Walker turned over his conversation with Truman. He'd been flattered to receive the invitation, welcomed into the former president's home, but what Truman said had unsettled him.

The talk felt less like nostalgia and more like a soft warning, and what Truman had said about Eisenhower disturbed Walker. He'd met Eisenhower, and thought of Ike as his own man, and not someone's dog to heel. Truman had implied otherwise. With Allen Dulles running the Company and John Foster Dulles heading State, the two brothers belonged to a fraternal tradition that included the Gracchi brothers, Frank and Jesse James, and the more recent examples of Robert and John Kennedy.

Walker remembered Eisenhower from when he and Jack had fought their way from France into Germany. There was white and there was red. Snow and blood. Flakes from above failed to cover the red beneath their boots. They'd arrived at a place where they found a different kind of ash, a human form of snow.

Dachau.

Ike had been at Ohrdruf, toured it with Generals Patton and Bradley. Eisenhower demanded that townspeople adjacent to the camps enter the facility, view the horrors, and bury the dead. He insisted the villagers see everything, and that everything be filmed for posterity.

Eisenhower wept in private. Patton threw up, and refused to enter one of the kill-sheds because the stench was far worse than any of the killing floors in an Upton Sinclair novel.

Walker had witnessed the aftermath of liberation in the death camp. Prisoners hunted down their former captors and beat them to death, with a rake, a shovel, or a trowel. They were not alone in their rage, as some of his fellow soldiers shot some of the SS on sight. Any guard foolish enough to change into the prisoner's uniform of striped cap, jacket, and pants to avoid detection met a worse fate; they were torn limb from limb, the inmates on him like ants on fallen food.

Walker had witnessed the unintended consequences of American kindness. Soldiers, eager to help, gave the starving men portions of their rations, unaware that, deprived of solid food for so long, their stomachs exploded and killed the inmate.

Mercy turned fatal. The righteous act, tragic.

And yet Truman had suggested that Eisenhower, who had stood amid the chaos and ruin, now danced to Dulles' tune.

It struck him as ironic, considering that 'Eisenhower' in German meant 'iron worker.'

Walker also couldn't ignore Truman's idea that the Company be led by military men who understood the cost of human life—yet Dulles was a civilian.

Walker parked the car. He observed a small child with a View-Master in the middle of the sidewalk. She held the toy up to the sky. The little girl clicked the lever to rotate whatever the wheel of pictures inside revealed. She clicked and clicked, frozen in place on the pavement, mesmerized and oblivious to the human traffic that teemed around her.

Each click, a chamber spun. Each glimpse, another fiction.

He imagined each pull of the lever as a trigger squeezed.

Each rotation, another round in the chamber. And each click, a lethal bullet spent.

Walker looked skyward.

It was thirty-six floors heavenward to meet Allen Welsh Dulles.

He hoped the bullets were still plastic.

Chapter Three

Walker strode across the polished mosaic floor, his shoes clicking sharply with each step. He flashed a smile at the man behind the Information Desk, ready to ask the important question. But before he could, the Answer Man said, "The express elevators behind you will take you to the thirty-sixth floor. When you get there, take a right."

The man's face was as neutral as Roman marble. Walker gave a brief nod, thanked him, and turned toward the eight bronze doors. Inside the elevator, he pressed the oval button, the sensation of weightlessness gripping his stomach as the car shot upward—different from his days of jumping out of planes. He watched the lights overhead, then the doors opened with a soft ping.

Cool air and dim light greeted him. He turned right, footsteps echoing as he walked towards the shaft of light at the end of the hallway. He passed desks, typewriters, scattered papers, the trappings of activity, but no one in sight.

A small mail tube. Mugs. Rubber stamps for something official. Ink pads.

A vending machine for cigarettes.

He knocked gently on the doorframe.

A man inside motioned for him to enter. "Please, have a seat."

Walker did, settling into the chair, his eyes saw the chessboard on the desk. It was a neat, old-fashioned set—wooden pieces, a worn board. The man opposite him noticed.

"You play?" he asked.

Walker chose silence. The man opposite offered a tight, knowing smile.

"The game of chess is excellent for learning about your opponent and yourself. My brother and I have come to anticipate each other's moves over the years." He paused. "How was your drive?"

"Fine, thank you."

"Sorry to hear the critics panned your play on the Rosenbergs."

"You can't please everyone."

"Always be suspicious of praise," Dulles quipped with a wry smile. "And what about your conversation with Truman?"

"Interesting."

"It always is." Dulles smiled again, his gaze sharp. "Was Honest Harry honest?"

Walker took a moment, studied the man. He assessed Dulles' subtle probing before he responded. "Let's just say his truths weren't always the whole picture."

"I like that." Dulles folded his hands in front of him. "What did Truman say about Eisenhower?"

Walker eyed Dulles carefully. "He implied…something more sinister. That Ike was more a puppet than a man of his own making."

Dulles nodded, his expression unreadable. "I understand. But the question remains: How much of that is truth, and how much is something else entirely? Politics is a game of perception."

Walker held back slightly, intrigued by Dulles' cryptic response. "Let's play, shall we?"

"Excuse me?"

"The art of conversation. It's the game we're both playing here."

"Ah," Dulles smiled, the faintest glimmer of approval in his eyes. "A gentleman's conversation. Evasive, elegant…and clever."

Walker raised an eyebrow. "You know, I expected you to be smoking a pipe."

Dulles hummed softly. "And betray my presence here with the fragrance of tobacco? I would've thought you learned that tidbit from Wild Bill himself, or from your lady friend Leslie. A scent betrays one's presence—like a fingerprint. As for my pipe, I reserve that for moments of solitude, when the workday is over. You understand, don't you?"

Walker nodded thoughtfully. He made a brief show of reading the office. "What is this place?"

"This," Dulles said, "used to be my office when this entire floor was home to the British Security Coordination. Familiar with the BSC?"

"Some. British propaganda ops on American soil, right?"

Dulles gave a small, dry smile. "Yes, but don't let the word propaganda sour your palate—it's just truth in a different suit."

"And the truth was what?"

"Eyes on the America First Campaign. The idea was to prevent U.S. involvement in the war. Lindbergh led the movement here, while Joe Kennedy championed isolationism abroad. But then Pearl Harbor happened, and the illusion crumbled."

Walker leaned forward slightly, his tone a little sharper. "If this was your office, you must be a master of accents, because you don't sound British to me."

Dulles's eyes sparkled something mischievous. "Didn't you know? I'm an excellent mimic. During my time here, I was the spy who spied on the spies."

Walker raised an eyebrow. "You spied on MI6?"

"I did. Colorful group. Graham Greene, Roald Dahl, and Ian Fleming, to name a few."

"Bond?" Walker smirked. "That 'license to kill' bit is a bit much, don't you think?"

Dulles moved a white piece on the chessboard. "You've read *Casino Royale?*"

"When it came out in April, yes."

"Well," Dulles said, "if you're fond of Fleming, I could get you an advance reader's copy of *Live and Let Die*. The publisher, Jonathan Cape, won't release it until next year." He moved a piece. "As for 'license to kill,' it wasn't all fiction, you know."

Walker narrowed his eyes, intrigued. "Authorized to kill on American soil?"

"When necessary," Dulles replied smoothly. He then reached into his pocket and pulled out a crisp, newly minted dollar bill. "Speaking of advanced information, I'd like to show you something," he said, pushing the bill across the desk. The reverse side displayed the Great Seal of the United States, and in bold new letters, the motto IN GOD WE TRUST.

Dulles tapped the motto with his finger. "This, Walker, is the future."

Walker examined the bill, his fingers brushing the paper. "The future of what?"

Dulles smiled, his gaze steady. "The future of a country that, with the right leadership, will outlast even the pyramids of Egypt."

"Is that so?" Walker muttered, his eyes on the bill. "We're Rome, and the rest of the world's what—barbarians?"

"We are," Dulles said softly, his smile never fading, "but greater. While Europe and Japan rebuild, our military becomes the strongest in history. As for Russia, Stalin is dead."

Walker's mind turned a page. "And the plan?"

"On paper, we seek oil from Iraq, Kuwait, and Saudi Arabia. In reality," Dulles paused, and the air grew still, "A coup."

Walker's eyes widened. "A coup?"

"To overthrow Mosaddegh and install the Shah."

Walker blinked, and the pieces began to fall into place. "You mean Mosaddegh signed his own death sentence when he nationalized Iran's oil?"

Dulles smiled. "That's one way of looking at it."

Chapter Four

K eys in one hand, Wayfarers in the other, Walker exited the building quickly, but not too quickly. He wanted distance between himself and Dulles.

At sixty, Dulles was still agile and cagey. He outmaneuvered attorneys, diplomats, even presidents. Like Cadmus, the bringer of civilization, Dulles sowed dragon's teeth and, like Jason, he knew how to defeat the stone warriors who rose from the soil.

He didn't dare use the nearest payphone, in case the Old Man had eyes on the street. Surveillance teams worked in pairs, all Company men, and rumor had it Dulles handpicked the darkest of horses for his personal detail. With sunglasses on, his eyes and emotions concealed, Walker scanned for any tourist who lingered too long.

Nothing.

Nobody.

He unlocked the door, slid in, turned the second key in the ignition. Let the car idle, let the air conditioning hum. He kept watch on the sidewalks and crosswalks. He searched for the inconspicuous man, the milquetoast man in a gray suit, dull tie, and pinched fedora.

He didn't rule out a female tail, but Dulles did. Women, in his view, were for sex and blackmail, the honeypot traps. Never fieldwork. Women to Dulles served as operators, secretaries, and the rare analyst. Leslie was that rare exception within the Company.

Dulles tolerated her only because she was legacy—an inheritance from General Walter 'Beetle' Smith. Dulles was known to keep bridges intact just long enough to burn them with the matchbook in his back pocket.

Walker assumed the Old Man had read every file the Company had on her. A man like Dulles never entered a building without knowing every entrance and exit. He must've seen her language credentials, her infiltration of Nazi Germany's upper ranks, and the methods she'd used to complete her assignments. Walker pictured Dulles setting aside his pipe so he could declare her a failure in intelligence because she had not succeeded in killing Hitler. The same Hitler Dulles had met in Berlin and later described to his brother Foster as 'not quite as bad' as people said. What Dulles failed to grasp was that Leslie's mission at the time was to eliminate one of Himmler's men and rescue a captured MI6 officer.

She'd once shown Walker a photo: Foster Dulles shaking Hitler's hand in 1933, with Allen lurking in the background. The Dulles brothers had an uncanny ability to separate Hitler's love of port and a good joke from his drive to turn his enemies to ash.

If Dulles thought little of Leslie, Walker suspected Jack Marshall fared worse, even though 'Wild Bill' Donovan recruited him. Donovan inspired loyalty of the most dangerous kind. His men would've followed him to Hell and back, which made him a threat to the status quo. His vision for American intelligence had rattled the old bureaucracies—Army G-2, Naval Intelligence, Hoover's FBI.

The knives came out. Generals Marshall and Strong sabotaged him with Lisbon. Hoover finished him off with gossip. A botched intercept and bedroom rumors were all it took to erase a war hero.

One hand on the oversized steering wheel, Walker reached for the radio dial. *Vaya con Dios* by Les Paul and Mary Ford played softly on the radio. His fingers brushed the cloth interior, and then he felt it—something solid and out of place. Glancing down, he saw a black View-Master, like the one he'd seen a child holding before he entered the building to meet Dulles. The photo wheel inside felt like a message, details of his mission hidden in the images.

Walker could either stay and be seen by whoever was watching him or drive off for a private show. He didn't want to be followed to a diner on the highway, so he picked up the child's toy and previewed the photo montage intended for him.

The sunlight and the solemn voices of the guitarist and the woman urging listeners to 'Go with God' set the scene as he clicked through the first of fourteen images.

He recognized the man in the bespoke suit: Shah Mohammad Reza Pahlavi; beside him, his wife, Soraya. The background suggested a major European city—likely Rome. The next photo was of another woman, strikingly similar to the Shah, enough to pass as his twin.

Walker clicked the lever. The next image showed Theodore Roosevelt. Then Kermit Roosevelt, Teddy's son, who committed suicide. The government told his mother he'd succumbed to a heart attack in Alaska. The next photo was of Kermit's son, Junior. 'Kim' Roosevelt was an expert on Arab-American Affairs, although Walker always thought it odd because Iranians weren't Arabs. They spoke Farsi, and the Shah's Peacock Throne traced its lineage to the Mughals in India.

Walker clicked through more stills: meetings between the Shah, Kim, and a third man. When the third man appeared alone, Walker was momentarily disoriented by his attire. He'd expected British tailoring—something he'd learned from his talks with Sheldon, a Company ally.

This man looked like any American college student, dressed in a parted hairstyle like Gene Kelly's, a shirt collar flared above a pullover sweater. Walker would've laughed at the idea that this was some ordinary College Joe, if he wasn't that much older than the 'kid' in the picture. Something about him said seasoned pro. Walker studied the body, the pose.

Norman Darbyshire, MI6's lead in Tehran, made sure to be photographed looking down, his hands at his sides—classic tricks to avoid identification. He worked the camera like Lombard had after a car accident had thrown her through a windshield. There was nothing to latch onto—not even an ear, which was as individual as a fingerprint.

Next came pictures of Sheldon: one in a suit, the other in casual clothes. The message was as clear as cancer on an X-ray. The suit wasn't just for style; it was a cover, and Dulles knew it. Sheldon had survived Auschwitz and dispensed his own form of justice to those the Nuremberg Trials had missed.

Walker clicked again, surprised to see Tania. She was an orphan, the victim of a sadistic man in Vienna. After Sheldon rescued her, she became fiercely loyal. She had tried to seduce Walker once. He rejected her, and she didn't forget it.

Tania was unlike Sheldon in one key way. She wasn't Jewish nor a camp survivor. Her father was a disillusioned communist in Budapest, sent to a Stalinist gulag, never to return. Her name, Tania, meant 'fairy queen' in Russian. Walker recalled Brahms' whorehouse, *Die Elfenkönigin Kuss*, or The Elf Queen's Kiss. Tania was capable of a magical kiss, though she'd sooner kill with an icicle.

A car horn blared, jarring him like a sharp gasp after being submerged underwater. He blinked, still processing the images. He forced his eyes back to the View-Master. The last image—his heart rate spiked.

This one wasn't just a photo. It was the message, sharp with teeth and a bite.

Whoever had assembled this knew him too well. Too neat. Too orchestrated. Too calculated. And now, whoever was watching was waiting for his next move.

Walker swallowed hard. His grip tightened on the wheel as the reality settled against his chest like cold steel. The game had changed.

A storm was coming, and he wasn't sure he could weather it.

Chapter Five

Walker had expected Betty Marshall to swing the front door open with a flashbulb smile and warm greeting. Instead, he stepped in and handed Jack the View-Master. If Jack was upset about the visit, he didn't show it. Walker had phoned from a filling station and kept the call short and cryptic. The door clicked shut behind him.

"You ought to be a spokesman for Triple A, with the mileage you've been putting on your car. What's with the toy?"

"Have a looksee."

"You were vague as gray on the phone."

"Ears might've been listening."

Jack understood. Operators still listened in, even if Ma Bell said otherwise. The Company had used Hello Girls to eavesdrop on calls—especially when foreign nationals were involved. And then there were the party lines. After the war, people had forgotten the old adage: Loose lips sink ships.

Walker mentioned the detour on the interstate that sent him to Manhattan, though he didn't say who he'd met at Rockefeller Center.

"Let's go into the other room," Jack said. Holding up the View-Master, "A picture is worth a thousand words, I suppose."

"More like pictures are war and peace."

Jack ushered Walker into the living room. To borrow a British phrase, Jack had 'moved house' from Georgetown to Cleveland Park for more space and better schools for Jack Jr. and Elizabeth. The six-bedroom Craftsman sat on the corner of Macomb and 35th, the only home in the neighborhood with a spacious backyard.

Walker asked for a glass of water. Jack pointed to the kitchen. Betty was out on errands. Walker heard the chain-pull of a lamp and the soft sigh of a cushion as Jack took his seat. In the kitchen, Walker ran the tap until the water turned cold. When he returned with a tall glass and coaster, Jack was already peering into the toy.

"This wasn't from Truman," Jack said. "He's out of the game."

"It's from the Old Man."

Jack lowered the View-Master. Two and two had come together.

"Dulles had you intercepted?"

* * *

"Met the man at Rockefeller Center. It was a curious conversation."

"Curious enough that you want to discuss it?"

"I'm used to a chain of command, Jack."

"But not used to someone taking a special interest?"

"This is Dulles."

"Understood," Jack said. "Let's start with Truman."

"You think the two are connected?"

"No coincidence he sent for you after meeting Truman. What was your read of Truman?"

Walker described Truman's piano, the song he'd played at Potsdam, the quip about politics and whorehouses. Jack listened. He knew Walker's memory was sharp, and he understood that with Dulles, every detail mattered.

"What do you make of it all?" Walker asked.

"I think you're holding something back, not that I think that's a bad thing." Jack paused. "My first thought is Truman's ego is talking."

Walker remembered: ego was not the same as egotism.

"His ego?"

"He's thinking of his legacy. The man created the Company, and now Dulles is running it in his own image. Disagree?"

"He seemed bothered a civilian is in charge."

"It's more than that."

"Truman made it sound like combat experience meant something."

"What's really bothering you, Walker?"

"It all felt like a warning."

Jack raised the View-Master. "And this confirms the fear?"

Walker stayed silent.

"Tell me about your encounter with Dulles."

Walker described the office, the BSC, its role during the war as a British outpost inside the American heart of corporate might and media. Churchill requested the placement, and Hoover had signed off. Eyes on eyes. Agencies sizing each other up like schoolboys—friends one day, adversaries the next. He left out the writers, but mentioned the chessboard.

Dulles had called Truman weak when Mosaddegh threatened to end foreign interference in Iranian politics as prime minister. Truman thought at the time that if he had Mosaddegh removed from office, it could delegitimize the Shah.

"Don't forget the Old Man's other concern," Jack said.

"Which is?" Walker asked.

"The Tudeh party."

Iran's Communists. Walker understood. "The Soviets would roll in and take the ports."

Jack finished the thought. "And control the Middle East."

Jack resumed his click-through of the View-Master. Walker drank deeply. After two long drives in a short window, he felt half-camel.

Jack set the toy aside. "Ideology motivates cooperation. Dulles is appealing to your patriotism, to stop Communism at all costs. But he left something out."

Jack explained how when Eisenhower took office, Dulles had Foster move an antitrust case against the Seven Sisters oil conglomerate from Justice to State, framing it as a national security issue.

"When Mosaddegh threatened to nationalize oil," Jack said, "Sullivan & Cromwell in London was tapped to broker a deal. The Dulles brothers are Sullivan & Cromwell. Moving the case to State made the deal bulletproof."

"And then Mosaddegh ruined everything."

"Everything is symbolic, Walker. The chessboard. That wasn't just decoration."

Jack didn't belabor the point. Truman's talk of Potsdam, Churchill, Stalin were all a baton pass. The old world yielding to a new one. Truman to Dulles. Dulles stated one truth: that the U.S. could replace Britain as the world's superpower, box in the Soviets, and become the quiet power behind the Peacock Throne.

"What really bothers you?" Jack asked.

"In so many words, he told me I'm the lead. You're not."

Jack didn't flinch. If anything, he relaxed.

"Congratulations, Walker."

"You're okay with a demotion?"

Jack replied calmly. "What did we learn in the Army?"

"This isn't the Army."

"What did we learn, Walker?"

"The mission comes first."

Jack held up the View-Master. "Think of it as a test."

"A test?"

"Does Walker have what it takes to be a Jack Marshall?"

"A case officer?"

Walker didn't want to admit it, but Jack was right. He may not have all the pieces or skills in place, but he had his senses, and they were heightened. Intuition was unreliable. Fear? Fear kept you alive. Paranoia was an asset.

"It's your decision."

"I suspect he'll send me to Switzerland. Dulles worked out of Bern."

"I would've guessed Germany. We've got Gehlen there."

"Switzerland has money. And neutrality."

"Does it matter?"

Walker stood. "I'll ditch this glass."

He used the walk to the kitchen to collect his thoughts. He had no sense whether Jack had been looped in, or how much. Dulles understood calculus, partial differentiation, the rate of change with respect to one variable while holding all other variables constant. Two years ago, Jack had worked Iran and Afghanistan. He was the logical choice to run the operation.

The kitchen layout was nearly identical to the old house. Same central table. Same Elmira fridge. He noticed a new cigarette brand. Betty had switched from Juleps to Lucky Strikes. He recalled Dulles's words about scent as signature.

As he returned to the living room, he passed the liquor cart.

"Noticed the Old Overholt Rye," Walker said.

"Stuff's harsh. I use it for a Manhattan or Vieux Carré."

"No Sazerac?"

"It's John Foster Dulles' favorite."

"You said everything's symbolic." Walker looked to the toy. "Talk to me about Kim Roosevelt."

"Met him when I was with Donovan. Before your time."

"Should I worry?"

"Kim cares about Kim."

"And the Shah?"

"Spineless. His sister's the one to watch."

"Norman Darbyshire?"

Jack leaned back. "Heard the name. First time I've seen a picture. He looks green."

"Looks like T.E. Lawrence before the costume change to me. You're the man for this job, Jack, not me."

"It's a test, like I said."

Walker stared. "He didn't say anything to you?"

"About you, no, though I was assigned a task."

"I guess we're both on a need-to-know basis."

"We all are with the Dulles brothers."

"Tell me about your task."

"Borscht Belt. I'm to have someone cultivate an asset there."

"Sheldon?"

"Makes the most sense," Jack said. "He's Jewish. He fits in where we don't. My guess is Dulles noticed Sheldon's involvement in the Rosenberg play. Along with Tania."

"Did he name the asset?"

Jack hesitated. "No," and he shifted in his seat. "You fine working with Leslie? She's the last picture in the carousel." Jack held up the View-Master. "You know why she's there, don't you?"

"She's British, former MI6, and Darbyshire is MI6. They know each other?"

"Knowing Dulles, also part of the test to see how you handle distraction. You two have history."

The front door unlocked. The jangle of housekeys.

Chapter Six

Betty entered the house, Elizabeth behind her, both Marshall women in mid-argument.

"You had no business being there."

"What's wrong with a cherry Coke at the soda fountain?"

"It's the crowd you've chosen for yourself, Elizabeth."

Metal met glass. Betty had tossed her keys; they clanged against the bowl on the hallway table, cluttered with mail, yesterday's paper, and the contents of emptied pockets. She and Elizabeth argued, their profiles a blur in the hallway's dim light, shadows on the wall. They were oblivious to Jack and Walker in the living room.

"And what's wrong with the girls I was with? There were no boys with us."

"Give the boys time, Elizabeth. Those girls are a bad influence."

"How can you say that? You're so unreasonable."

"Stop being so dramatic, Elizabeth."

"I have no friends in this godforsaken village."

"Village?"

"Be serious, Mother. This burg hasn't changed since Thornton Wilder's *Our Town*."

"Nice to hear you're awake in class. Let's hope your grades from Miss Rittenauer reflect it."

"You talked to my homeroom teacher? The school year hasn't started, and you're already spying on me?"

"Enough of the melodrama, Elizabeth. It's unbecoming."

Elizabeth threw her hands in the air. "Oh, but it's not beneath my own mother to be on the lookout for juvenile delinquents at the local soda fountain."

"I didn't call anyone a delinquent. I just wish you would exercise some discernment."

"I take it back."

"Take what back?"

"This isn't *Our Town*. It's *Spoon River*. I might as well be living inside a snow globe—everything's frozen and everyone's pretending to be cheerful."

Betty paused, perplexed. "I don't get the reference."

"Weren't you awake in class, in the last century?"

Jack had had enough and did the clichéd cough to announce his presence. His wife and daughter turned their heads as if they were deer on the lawn, seen but not startled.

"Ladies."

"Jack," Betty said, automatically smoothing the front of her dress. She noticed Walker and almost transformed into the perfect hostess. Elizabeth, however, walked the short distance to Walker and kissed him on the cheek. "Hello, Walker."

"And now, say goodbye to Walker." Jack's eyes motioned toward the kitchen.

Elizabeth did a slow walk, glancing over her shoulder.

Walker whispered to Jack. "I don't envy you."

"Makes shooting Fritzes seem like a garden party, doesn't it?"

Betty strode up to Jack, abrupt as a drill sergeant. "You need to speak to your daughter. I found her at Stark's with the wrong crowd."

"There's a wrong crowd? You just happened to see her at the counter as you drove by?" Jack raised an eyebrow and then looked at Walker. "Where was she when we needed a sniper?"

"I'm serious, Jack."

Jack held up his hands. "As am I, Betty, but cut the girl some slack. It's a new town, new high school. She's trying to make friends before school starts."

"She's at a dangerous age," Betty said, her hands now firmly on her hips.

"And what does that mean?"

"Where there are flowers, there's honey."

Jack turned to Walker. "Let's continue our talk at Martin's."

Betty moved when Jack moved. "Don't you run away, Jack Marshall."

"Answer me this, Betty. Liz accused you of spying. Were you, yes or no?"

"No."

"You miraculously happened to be in the right place at the right time? I must be mistaken, because it feels like this chapter reads like one of those novels where the main character meets all the important people in history."

"What are you saying?"

"I'm saying how convenient it was for you to drive past Stark's and see Liz."

"If you must know, I was on my way to Wilson for a meeting."

Jack's forehead creased. "Isn't it a bit premature for a PTA meeting?"

"Not the PTA. The Community Coordinating Council."

Jack seemed to relax. "The library committee?"

"No, the WISE program." Betty's voice was colder now.

Jack blinked. "What the hell is WISE?"

"An initiative for integrated education."

"As in mixing races?"

"The ladies on the planning committee are drafting a proposal for funding from George Washington University to welcome black children into the elementary and high schools. I've discussed this with you, but it seems you weren't listening."

"I listen, Betty." Jack took her arm and moved her away from Walker. "We'll talk about this later. Please keep the peace while I'm out."

"Where are you going?"

"Martin's. I won't be long. I need to speak with Walker."

Betty removed her gloves, one finger at a time, pinning Jack with a glare for each digit.

* * *

In the driveway, Jack searched his pocket for his keys.

"Word of advice, friend. Think twice about marriage."

"Under advisement," Walker replied, leaning against the hood of the Bristol 403.

Jack turned the engine over, and they backed out of the driveway. "It's not that I regret it, but I swear my hair will either turn gray or fall out. I don't know which first."

"Trouble with Jack Junior?"

"The kid's fine. He listens when I talk."

"But not Elizabeth?"

"She listens, but takes everything I say as a personal challenge."

"I don't know who's got it worse—you with them, or me with Dulles."

During the ten-minute drive to Martin's Tavern, Walker took in the tree-lined streets of Cleveland Park. The neighborhood looked like a postcard, suburban calm minutes away from the nation's capital. Jack had picked it for sanctuary—a place for his son to earn varsity letters and for Elizabeth to live out a high school fantasy in a poodle skirt, corsage on her wrist.

They passed a house where a pair of sheep grazed in the yard.

Jack caught Walker's glance. "Don't ask."

"Town eccentric?"

"Something like that."

Jack parked on Wisconsin, and they made their way into Martin's Tavern. He asked for a booth in the Dugout Room. Behind them, a couple requested Booth Three—the so-called Proposal Booth. They'd read somewhere that John F. Kennedy had proposed to Jackie there, June 24, 1953. Jack resisted the urge to debunk it. He knew better. There were two other claimants to that story, both in Boston: Table 40 at the Parker House and a corner booth at Locke-Ober. Kennedy had been seeing doctors in Boston that June for his back. Jack had the names of those doctors, courtesy of J. Edgar Hoover.

As they slid into their booth, Walker raised an eyebrow. "Why this place, Jack?"

"To be seen and overheard."

After their drinks arrived, Jack raised his glass. "To dull, duller, and Dulles."

"May they see us, but not hear us."

They sipped. Jack's expression shifted. "You don't have to take the assignment."

"Wouldn't it be bad form to refuse?"

"Depends on whether you want to stay with the Company."

"I'm not sure I've got the stomach for it." Walker looked down.

"The first time as a Case Officer is the hardest. But if it works, it changes everything."

"And if it doesn't?"

"Then we blame the British. But we both know what's at stake."

Walker nodded, feeling the weight settle. "And if it really goes south?"

"More bodies for Arlington. Either way, the show goes on. Food?"

They ordered, and the waitress returned with their drinks. Walker sipped a dark Mexican lager. A light foam clung to his lip, and he wiped it away with a napkin. "No matter how much we argue, Sheldon's the key, isn't he?"

Jack nodded. "Do your part, I'll do mine."

"I'd like to know who this asset is in the Borscht Belt."

"Let me worry about that. Stop chewing your tail. Trust us to do our part."

"But the Borscht Belt, Jack. I don't know. Unknown territory."

"So was L.A., and you managed fine. Think of the Belt as a back channel. You handle foreign. I'll handle domestic."

Walker sensed a weight behind Jack's words—something personal.

"Something on your mind?"

"I never asked this before. Are you religious?"

"Lapsed Catholic. You?"

"Montana Methodist."

Walker gave him a look. "What's with the strange question?"

Jack hesitated. "Something I saw at the office."

"Dulles'?"

Jack shook his head. "No. Angleton's office."

Walker sat up straighter. "Angleton?"

"Yeah." Jack leaned in, voice low. "His door was open. The Ghost was kneeling."

"Praying?"

Jack nodded. "Like he was in a confessional. His middle name's Jesus. What does that tell you?"

Walker paused. "And that worries you?"

"Not exactly. But it unsettles me. Makes me think of when faith starts steering the wheel instead of the Constitution."

Walker looked down at his beer. "The Founding Fathers knew a thing or two about spycraft, but they didn't imagine atomic bombs, fallout shelters, or the Company."

"And then there's Dulles and his chessboard."

Chapter Seven

From Union Station to Chicago, with a connection to New York, the walls of the LA Limited shuddered as the lights flickered. A freight train on the opposite track cast a rhythmic play of light and shadow on the glass.

An hour earlier, a Lothario had gawked at her with all the finesse of a door-to-door salesman. He tried out a few lines; she batted her eyelashes, playing along just enough to deflect his awkwardness. She looked away, but he didn't take the hint—an inexperienced college boy who believed dressing like his father made him mature. The open collar of his blue Arrow shirt, the color choice meant to seem bold, the carefully styled quiff—all, in his mind, marked him as a rebel. Not those clothes, and not with that hair, she thought. He still had a lot to learn about what makes a man. And she left him behind.

When she heard the door open and close behind her, she smiled and shook her head. He deserved an A for persistence. Crossing one leg over the other, she waited for the next pitch. She promised herself she'd be merciful, remembering her own rehearsals for adulthood. But that had been before the war: first in England, where class defined everything, then in France and Germany, where her charm served the British SOE, the Special Operations Executive.

That was then. This was now. She was in America—and this young man was no Nazi.

He asked if he could join her. At last, she relented, and he sat across from her.

He reached into his jacket. She expected a pack of cigarettes, but instead pulled out a silver clamshell case. He opened it and offered her one. She shook her head.

She noticed the French cuffs, the initials FG on the cufflinks. He closed the case without taking one for himself, which relieved her. The last thing she wanted was a re-creation of that scandalous scene from *Now, Voyager*—him as Paul Henreid, her as Bette Davis. He'd light a cigarette, then pass it to her in a sublime act of seduction. It was the move that launched a thousand cigarettes for Casanovas and their conquests.

"Traveling alone?" he asked, eager to keep the game going.

"Observant," she said, playing along. Her eyes flicked to the passing landscape outside the window, but she could feel his gaze following her every move.

"I saw you in the dining car," he said with a smirk, his voice too self-assured for someone so unsure.

He exercised male prerogative. His eyes started with her shoes and worked their way up to her eyes. The slow crawl was his idea of subtle. She barely stopped herself from rolling her eyes. She tolerated it.

"You're not what I expected," he said finally.

"And what did you expect?" she asked, raising an eyebrow.

"High heels," he said, glancing at her feet. "Not flats."

"It's called comfort for travel."

"What about those slacks?"

Her eyes met his. "What about them?"

"Mother said trousers are for housework."

"Ah, invoking mother." She smiled. "Not gonna help your cause. If she's who comes to mind, I suggest the analyst's couch."

He waved a finger at her, almost wagging it. "Feisty."

"If you think that's feisty, you should try me after my second cup of coffee. Which college do you attend?" she asked, curious.

He parted his jacket, giving a dramatic glance to his left and right, as if expecting her to be impressed. "Something about me say I'm a man about campus?"

She studied him for a moment, and the corners of her lips curled. "I don't see a wedding band, or the telltale signs of someone who's taken it off. The question is—Windy City or Big Apple? And why the hurry?"

He smirked and shook his head. "Have it your way," he said, no longer playing along.

She said, "Let's play this as if we're in a movie."

"Which one?"

"I was thinking, *Strangers on a Train*."

"But that was with two guys," he countered, surprised. "And you're no guy."

She leaned back. "You really know how to compliment a lady."

He shifted uncomfortably under her gaze. "Does the lady have a name?"

"Margaret, or you can call me Maggie. And you?"

"Paul."

She glanced down at his sleeve. "It doesn't match the initial F on the cufflinks."

"What can I say? I improvised." He laughed nervously, avoiding eye contact.

"If you're going to lie to someone, don't have any evidence around to trip you up."

"Seems like you don't mind lies."

"Everyone lies, Paul, or is it Frank?"

He puffed his chest, clearly eager to come up with something impressive. "It's Franklin. Not exactly a name with wow, is it?"

"Blame mom or dad for that?"

"Mom."

"I was right. There's a psychoanalyst couch in your future."

"If I had had my choice, I would've preferred the name Finn."

"Huck it is. I'm Maggie, if you haven't heard. What do you study?"

"Father wants me to be an engineer."

"And what does mom want?" she asked, leaning in slightly, her voice softer now.

"She wants me to be happy. She's convinced I can do anything, but..." He trailed off, suddenly vulnerable. "But I'm not sure if I can deliver the order from the menu. Sometimes I wonder if I'm just doing what I'm told, not what I really want to do." He paused, looking out the window for a moment. "You know, like… can you ever just be enough for everyone, or do you have to be something else?"

She studied him for a moment, wondering what had led to the sudden vulnerability. He was young, full of bravado, yet there was a flicker of doubt, the scared little boy behind his eyes. "You'll figure it out, Franklin. But right now, you need to stop overthinking and enjoy the moment. A lot of people get stuck in their heads like that. You're lucky you're young enough to still choose."

He gave a small, almost relieved laugh. "That might be the best advice anyone has given me." He leaned forward, earnest. "Hey, stranger on a train, answer me this question."

She didn't say a word. She waited.

"Most women wear gloves, white ones, but you don't. Don't tell me it's because you're not most women and because it's summer."

"Which do you want to hear, Franklin?" He pulled his head back, confused. She said, "The truth or the lie?"

He shrugged. "The truth, always, why?"

"The truth or a lie, both make men run."

"I was asking about gloves, and nothing Freudian about the color either."

"I wear gloves when I don't want to leave fingerprints behind."

"No fingerprints." He laughed. "That's rich," he said and waved his finger at her. "I'll remember that one. This has been fun, and I'm a good-enough sport to concede defeat. This has been swell."

She watched him walk away. He seemed pleased with himself. She heard him open the door to the next car and watched him disappear into the next compartment. If only he knew that she had told the truth, that it hadn't been a lie. The last time someone had run away from her was in a forest. At a respectable distance, she'd shot a Nazi, with his own Luger. She had enjoyed their fight, so she'd toyed with him. As he crawled around in the dirt, wounded, she walked over to him, tipped him over with her boot so he could see her.

She remembered well how the German pistol had kicked under the recoil when she delivered the final and fatal shot. She tossed the pistol onto his chest and left the scene wearing gloves.

White gloves, like a lady would.

Chapter Eight

The phone rang in Boston. Sheldon answered. Jack's voice traveled up the coast from D.C. His voice was smooth, diplomatic. A job in the Catskills, he said.

But Sheldon didn't work for thirty pieces of silver, and Jack knew it. He wanted justice. Jack promised him the name of a war criminal in hiding. And that promise stood, no matter how the Catskills turned out.

"Why me?" Sheldon asked.

Jack told him. He gave the expected line: nobody available on short notice, nobody who could pass for Jewish. He hesitated. "No one ethnic enough."

"Ethnic," Sheldon repeated, laughing. "Next word out of your mouth'll be swarthy."

To the world, Jews were the red-headed Judas. Christ-killers. Shylock.

The "Dirty Hebe" in Hitler's cartoons. Words he had heard all his life.

Now, with McCarthy hunting Reds in closets and under beds, they were cast again—as suspicious intellectuals or, worse, as Communists, un-American to the core.

'Swarthy' was just one more insult on a long list.

Sheldon asked what he should do with Tania if he took the assignment. If Sheldon's looks were what the director ordered, hers came from the bottom of the deck. She wasn't Jewish, and she didn't pass for American. She was what fashion magazines called striking—tall and lanky, platinum-blonde, with a Botticelli body and a cold, European kind of glamour.

Infiltrating a resort in the Catskills would be easy. The rest wouldn't.

Jack gave Sheldon a name—one Dulles hadn't passed along to Walker.

Dulles wanted to see how resourceful Walker would get to complete the job. Jack thought what Dulles did was dirty. In the Army, orders were given face-to-face or through the chain of command, over maps and mud. In the Company, they were knives in sealed envelopes. Walker would have to learn that.

Jack explained to Sheldon what the man had that the Company needed, and, knowing Sheldon was a tailor by trade, he didn't dress it up: nobody had any idea what the man wanted in return.

Jack suggested Tania play niece. A bachelor would raise eyebrows in a family-oriented place. If Sheldon were younger, his presence wouldn't have turned heads. But he was thirty-three. Sheldon looked older. Life in Auschwitz had carved long lines into a face that said camp survivor.

Sheldon glanced over at Tania. She was reading a book. Before hanging up the phone with Jack, he'd promised to talk to her. She'd make her own decision.

Tania consumed books in several languages. She'd devoured the French version of Yourcenar's *Memoirs of Hadrian* in days. Her command of German was second only to Russian, and her love of Slavic literature ran deep. She'd tried American authors, but despaired. Holden Caulfield was insufferable. Lately, she'd been obsessed with Baldwin and Ellison.

Tania wasn't the feral child of Vienna anymore, but her ferocity remained. She demonstrated it when one of Roy Cohn's associates had kidnapped and abused her. Her skirmishes with authority were minor but noteworthy. Like the time Sheldon enrolled her in a private girls' school run by a Catholic order. Her father a communist atheist, Tania was areligious. The details were murky, but a nun had struck her with a ruler. Tania retaliated. Where there once was white in the woman's habit, there was now red from all the blood.

The nuns didn't know, nor could they have known, that she'd been raped in Vienna. Repeatedly. She'd come to know darkness in others and herself. Her name in Russian meant 'fairy queen,' and it fit. She understood the dark woods around her. She observed, assessed every creature within reach, listened to her own tenebrous heartbeat.

* * *

While Sheldon drove his silver Nash-Healey down the interstate highway, she was reading James Baldwin's *Go Tell It on the Mountain*.

"How much longer, Uncle Shelly?"

"An hour, not much more." She closed the book. He'd noticed. "Any good?"

"It's interesting, although I don't understand the American fascination with religion."

"Religion provides comfort, structure, and it has a strong presence in Negro culture."

"Former slaves adopted the religion of their oppressors. Marx was right; it is an opiate."

Sheldon could have sighed the sigh of exasperation, a mimic of teens and adolescent drama, but he didn't. Tania was different. She didn't care what people thought of her, and God Himself help the fool who'd try to tell her what to do and what to think.

Sheldon reached out with his hand for hers. She flipped her hand over and accepted his.

"I think it's unwise to bring Marx into conversation these days." He squeezed her hand and changed tack. "I appreciate your coming with me."

"What else was I going to do?"

"Maybe, start to think about college. You're eighteen," Sheldon answered. "There are plenty of excellent schools for women in Massachusetts."

"Is that why you choose to live in Boston?"

"I would be lying if I didn't."

"Thank you for thinking ahead."

Sheldon bypassed the potential for sentimentality. "There's Mount Holyoke, Radcliffe, Smith, and Wellesley." The forefinger of his hand on the wheel indicated the road ahead of them. "If you like New York, there's Barnard and Vassar."

"Why else did you choose Massachusetts?"

"It's a liberal and progressive state—tolerant compared to others."

She smiled. "Tolerant isn't a word that I'd associate with the Puritans, considering how the colonists treated Indians. The other day, I was reading about a Massachusetts regiment that refused to join a regiment from New York because of the 'Fenian element.'"

"Never said history was pleasant." Sheldon tried to revisit his topic. "About college—"

"You assume I'll get into any of those schools."

Now, he sighed. A moment of quiet self-doubt. "You have the grades, Tania."

"And the black marks, and the demerits. I'm a woman without qualities."

"Clever allusion to Musil's novel, Tania, but you need not worry over a few mishaps."

"A few?"

Sheldon stared ahead at the asphalt and open sky. "Is youthful indiscretion a better phrase? Nothing a generous donation won't solve."

"I forgot," she said. "Money solves and absolves. I have a question for you."

"Why don't I like the sound of this?" He checked the side mirror. "What is it?"

"At this resort, am I to remain quiet when they discuss *Diary of a Young Girl?*"

"And why do you think the book will come up in conversation?"

"You know it'll come up. The book is all the rage, and consider the audience."

Sheldon couldn't look at her, but he could feel her eyes on him. She had had her horrors at the hands of men, and he'd been forced to participate in an unspeakable atrocity. She'd endured the worst of violence men could impose on a woman's body and spirit. He helped erase his own people. He tried to respect her nightmare, finding it ironic that German shared the same word for the experience: *das Trauma*, neuter, as in neutral and irrespective of gender.

"And why do you feel compelled to comment on it?"

"Anne Frank didn't survive, but I did."

"It's not the same thing, Tania."

"I know it's not. But sometimes it feels like the world made her a symbol so it wouldn't have to face the rest of us."

Sheldon's mind flashed to the children he escorted into the gas chambers, innocents who had no idea what was to come. He had hoped it was painless. He knew it often wasn't.

"Because I'm not Jewish, is that it?"

"Some Jews may think that, yes."

"They don't know what the Nazis did to Russians."

Sheldon didn't disagree with her about Hitler's hatred for Slavs. He'd experienced firsthand the suspicion from other survivors when they found out that he was a *sonderkommando*, part of the work detail who escorted prisoners into the gas chambers and removed their bodies for the crematoria. Many considered work crews complicit, though they didn't know that the Nazis liquidated them, so there would be no evidence of genocide.

"Anne Frank was different," he said.

"Different how, Uncle Shelly?"

"*Sie ist unberührbar.*"

"She was untouchable? Nobody is untouchable."

"That's exactly why her story matters," he said quietly. "Because people wanted to believe she was."

Her comment had been pointed, and Sheldon knew it. What she said without saying was that he had the ability to reach out and have others feel his touch, and when many former Nazis departed from this world, the last image they saw was Sheldon.

"I don't think her diary tells the whole truth," she said.

Sheldon still held her hand. "I'm sure liberties were taken, but the horror is the same."

"I wonder if she would've written it the same way if she'd lived," Tania said. "If she could've looked back without anyone editing her voice."

"She was sixteen."

"Exactly. And still real. Real girls are angry. Real girls have secrets. They fall in love. They think about their bodies. Don't you think it matters that we remember her as she really was, not just as a symbol of innocence?"

"Tania, please. This is different. The world needs Anne Frank."

"Maybe. But it also needs the ones like me—who weren't innocent, who weren't protected, who weren't written about."

"It's important that someone remember the dead, Tania. It's why Kaddish is said."

"'Humankind cannot bear very much reality,' especially in America."

"And she quotes T.S. Eliot to me."

"Anything you think I should remember while I'm there?" she asked.

"While we are there, please don't talk to me in German or Russian."

She looked out the window. "German because of the Nazis? They must know that Yiddish is a dialect of German, along with other languages, don't they?"

"Of course they do, Tania, but it takes time to heal. Life is still raw."

She squeezed his hand. "I understand why you don't want me to speak Russian, but it's hard for me. You help keep the language alive when we talk."

"I know. You do the same for me."

Chapter Nine

Trains inbound to Grand Central Station emptied out into a reception area the locals called the Kissing Room. Walker witnessed no smooches here. None. Rules were printed, framed, and mounted on a wall close to him. Boyfriends and girlfriends, husbands and wives, Jezebel and her victim, and a man and his mistress had to obey them.

No kiss could last longer than five seconds.

None of the steamy stuff.

Absolutely nothing French.

And only in the Kissing Gallery.

Uniformed staff patrolled the room like proctors at a high school dance. Whether it was a Kiss and Hi, or Kiss and Bye, modesty had to be maintained, and Ecclesiastics got it right, about a time and place for everything. Walker thought, and yet here he was, caught in this moment, more Hamlet than Romeo.

To kiss or not to kiss Leslie—that was the question when she walked off the Lake Shore Limited, her connection out of Chicago to New York. He saw the train, heard the brake gasp, and the conductor announce the stop. A brigade of porters, black men in white shirts, dark slacks, and hats, unloaded parcels and suitcases. He could spot Midwesterners from a mile away, a tribe he had once belonged to, years ago. He'd come to admire their innocence, the brightness in their smiles, and their gleam of hope that New York was just another field of promise they could harvest. But he knew the darker side of Middle America, too—had wondered if it was where the Fourth Reich would rise, speaking English. It was in the land of golden wheat and corn that they declared Roosevelt a traitor to his class, branding him a communist, and businessmen called the government socialist. He read articles about how children danced in the fields the day Roosevelt died.

From thirty feet away, he recognized her gait. It was unmistakable—her movement said she was carrying. His guess was a .22 caliber pistol, a gift from the Maquis when she'd worked with the French Resistance. The weapon, a quiet but lethal reminder of the past, had a red Croix de Lorraine on the white enamel grip. Feminine. Deadly. Like her lipstick.

In a three-quarter-sleeve polka dot dress, with a small carry case on wheels behind her, Leslie traveled light and in comfort. Flats instead of heels. The dark band on her straw sunhat matched the dots. He stood tall for her to see him, though she'd probably spotted him from inside the car.

She approached, and he noticed her eyes drift eastward. A young man nodded to her and went on his way.

"Isn't he a bit young, even for you?" Walker said.

She leaned in and kissed him on the cheek. "He's a kid, and you're a man."

He enjoyed the compliment, the warmth of her breath against his cheek. Leslie didn't wear perfume. Dulles was right; it betrayed presence. Where most women wanted to be seen and remembered, Leslie preferred anonymity.

"The Biltmore is behind us," he told her. "No need to go outside, into the heat."

"Is that what is called a Manhattan transfer?"

"It's not just the name of a novel."

"You can't help but be literary," she said as they walked across the hard stone, her feet silent. "Which reminds me, have you written anything lately?"

"Wouldn't you like to know?" he said, with a little smirk. "Your room is on the smaller side. I hope you don't mind."

"It's not like I'm staying in it for long. When is our flight?"

"Tomorrow. He said we'd be in Bern by early afternoon."

"When did Jack tell you that?"

Walker sensed something in her tone. "Last night, why?"

Leslie smiled as the elevator doors opened. They stepped inside. The attendant held the door, and Walker let her exit first. She waited for him, until the door closed behind them.

"I was told Rome."

"Not by Jack, I presume."

"Correct."

Walker shook his head. "Someone overrode Jack?"

"Are you surprised?"

"No," he said. "So much for the chain of command."

They proceeded to the hotel's main counter, where a clerk with wattage for a smile awaited. Walker stepped back with a brochure in his hand while Leslie checked in. He skimmed the amenities. The Biltmore Hotel offered guests a writing space in each room, and a larger one for men on the southern half of the ground floor. Women had theirs in the northern section. The place felt like an historical potpourri of decoration—Elizabethan dark oak furniture, gold decorations, and red carpeting from the Baroque, and a Mediterranean touch with palm trees and a skylight.

Leslie declined the assistance of a bellhop. She returned to Walker, who had been surveying the lobby.

On the carpet of some royal scene from a medieval tapestry, they walked a short distance. Walker would've said something, but he felt that she had the upper hand about their itinerary, so he refrained from asking about their true destination. But she saved him from the agony.

"We're to go to the Excelsior Hotel in Rome."

"I'll take Italy before Switzerland," Walker said, his voice a little sharper than intended.

"It's not like choosing between the Yankees and the Dodgers."

"I take it that you haven't seen Brooklyn."

"No, but I'll take Brooklyn over Bern any day," she said, her voice laced with humor.

Whether it was the old man's former office at Number 23 Herrengasse in Bern or the Excelsior, both were Dulles territory. The old man used Rome as a base for his not-so-clandestine affairs. Whether he was the conqueror or conquered, the latest rumor with legs in DC was that the married Dulles and

Clare Boothe Luce were the subject of conversations behind closed doors and over cocktails at midnight.

"Any guess as to why Rome?" Walker asked.

She whispered, "Dulles frequents the bar while his wife shops the Via Veneto."

"He brought the wife this time?" Walker asked.

"Does it matter? Clover knows all about his assignations."

Clover was the nickname for Dulles' wife, Martha Todd.

"An affair sounds like a liability to me," Walker said.

"Affairs," Leslie said, "The old man is a prolific repeat offender." She gave a light touch to his arm, stopping him. "That's where he's ingenious. Remember the 20th of July?"

Walker's eyes flickered with recognition. "The plot to assassinate Hitler?"

"A mistress leaked it to Dulles." Leslie continued before he could ask who she was and how she came to be at the right place at the right time. "Mary Bancroft. Worked for Donovan's OSS. They rendezvoused in Switzerland."

"Gives new meaning to 'ride a desk,'" Walker said, his face pink.

"Their relationship cooled off, but not before Bancroft and Clover became close friends."

"Friends, huh?" Walker said, eyebrow raised. "And people say liberal is a bad word."

"I think those two would've called their arrangement modern or enlightened. The point is that his extramarital affairs are a matter of public record, so it negated the possibility of blackmail."

Walker asked, "And we should expect Clare on his arm in Rome?"

"Maybe or maybe not," Leslie said, adding that Eisenhower had made Clare Boothe Luce Ambassador to Italy, and no doubt the devout Catholic would provide Dulles with a direct line of communication to the pope. The Italians resisted at first but took to her, calling her La Signora.

"A convenient and strategic bedmate to have, don't you think?" Walker said, his voice low but thoughtful.

He meant that the old man's playmate was married to the man who had founded the magazines *Fortune, Life,* and *Time.* Clare Boothe Luce and Allen

Dulles, Leslie explained, shared a love of Princeton in New Jersey, where she staged her plays. She had already established her name on Broadway with the smash play *The Women* and as an editor of *Vanity Fair*.

"And I thought," Walker said, "affairs were about sex, not alliances."

"Everything in intelligence is a strategy. Sex, if it happens, is a benefit." Leslie smiled the smile of a mischievous pixie. Walker wondered if she considered him an alliance—or a casualty.

"His most brilliant partnership isn't with a woman, though," Leslie said, letting the statement linger. "You have yet to meet Edward Bernays."

"Not a name I know, Leslie."

"You will. He's the man who shapes the public's perception, from the brand of soap to buy to influencing entire nations. If you think Dulles is the architect of global manipulation, you're wrong. Bernays built the foundation. He wrote the book on mass persuasion, how to bend minds and hearts with nothing but words. Bernays wrote the textbook; Dulles, the playbook."

Walker nodded slowly, absorbing the weight of her words. "And I suppose you see yourself as someone who's followed the playbook?"

Leslie smiled, a glint in her eyes. "Think of it as a playbill."

Walker raised an eyebrow. "We are actors and this is grand theater."

"And Bernays is America's Prospero."

Leslie looked at Walker, her expression changing subtly. "We had a conversation in Vienna."

He said nothing.

"I'd suggested that you walk away from all of this. Remember?"

"I recall that it was more of a suggestion than advice. You told me to go off and become a writer." He could see sadness in her eyes. "I don't live in the past, Leslie. I came to respect why you chose this life, and I ask that you do the same with me now." He tapped her shoulder. "The way you're talking makes it seem as if my soul is in jeopardy. I wouldn't have counted you among the religious."

"I'm not," she said, "as for damnation, remember that Dulles will know you're dead before the devil does."

They entered another elevator, told the attendant the floor.

Walker asked, "How is Vera?"

Leslie glanced sideways. "I heard she was well."

Walker's voice lowered. "You haven't talked to her?"

She didn't answer right away. "It's been a while."

They arrived and stepped out into the hallway. They waited until the doors to the elevator had closed. Leslie stood firm as a soldier, but there was a flicker of something raw behind her eyes. "You have me if you want me, Walker—but I won't beg, and I won't say it again." She paused, long enough for him to feel the history between them. "If I don't interest you anymore, just say so. Don't make me guess."

He kissed her, and the kiss violated all the rules. It lasted more than five seconds, included some steam, and his caress and her response suggested that they'd take it inside. The door could say it was noiseless, but they wouldn't be.

Chapter Ten

Walker was not impressed with what he saw outside the window of their hired car on the drive to the hotel in the Roman neighborhood of Ludovisi. He'd once read somewhere that when Goethe had visited Rome, he found a city overrun with weeds, its great monuments a battleground between cats and vermin. The outskirts reminded Walker of Gower Gulch in LA, back when he was writing scripts for Jack Warner. Shabby, desolate, and devoid of life. Whole stretches of land were perfect for B-films and C-list actors. Leslie, sitting beside him, was silent as a stoic.

In Rome, there were signs of revival, slow but certain. Once a Purgatory for prisoners after the war, Cinecittà was rising from the muddy waters of the Tiber River as the new Hollywood. Mussolini's corpse had long since swung from a hook in Milan, a distant memory. Fascists had been forgiven. Italy had remained intact, a prize for the victorious Americans to control a battered Europe and counter the growing Soviet threat.

They walked into the Hotel Excelsior on Via Veneto, a street the length of two American football fields, lined with chic restaurants and sleek shops. Gossip and new money glistened like diamonds. Stars and starlets from Hollywood scandals roamed freely, while financiers dropped cash on haute couture. Noblemen with titles as worthless as their villas turned gigolo to pay the bills.

Veneto was too short a street for Allen Welsh Dulles, the Presbyterian from Watertown, to spend his holidays at the Excelsior. But when he wasn't at the embassy down the road, he'd meet with men who had helped him undermine the 1948 Italian elections in Room 128. The spymaster sipped martinis in the bar on lazy afternoons.

Dulles kept active. Dulles kept spry. The serpent never lacked charm in the garden.

The man behind the desk moved his eyes in a way that suggested Walker was less of a man because Leslie did all the talking, her Italian crisp as a starched collar. She held the double letters tight and together, making it clear her facility with the language wasn't from a Berlitz guide.

Once inside their room, Walker opened the doors to the balcony to let in some air. He noticed the stack of complimentary newspapers on the desk and ran his foot along the floor, searching for an uneven spot. Finding one, he moved the chair into position. Leslie unpacked her clothes in silence. Walker perused a British paper. "That was emasculating downstairs," he said, tossing the paper aside.

"Why would you need to learn Italian unless you're an art historian or musician?"

"Is that your reminder that your British education is superior to mine?" Walker shot back.

"Defensive, are we? Americans are pragmatic. They study French."

"To be or not to be the hairy ape abroad...or speak the language of diplomacy."

She shot him a look over her shoulder. "Hairy Ape?"

"A play by Eugene O'Neill."

Walker flipped through more pages. "I'm the monolingual Cyclops. The proverbial ugly American."

"Spare me the self-pity. You're not ugly, Walker."

"A *bracco italiano* is a hound, right?"

Her eyebrows pinched. "A pointer, why?"

"That's me. I'll point at the menu and drool."

She folded her evening wear. "Anything in the paper worth more than three lire?"

Walker turned the paper around and tossed it on the bed for her to see. "Lead story is some guy died last year. Family wants to turn his stores into a retail chain. Food was his specialty. Negotiations between a buyer and his family have gone nowhere."

"Name of the family?"

"Caprotti."

Leslie smiled as she hung up a blouse.

"What's so funny? Did I mispronounce it?" Walker asked.

"Caprotti means 'goatherder.' And your vowels could use some work. You'll need to hold the double consonants for a beat," she said, demonstrating with 'bruschetta,' 'gnocchi,' and 'prosciutto.' He tried to imitate her, and thought of what Dulles said about his skill as a mimic. She dismissed his efforts with a wave. "Forget the lesson. Tell me who's investing in a dead man's business."

"Nelson Rockefeller. Why?"

"Read between the lines, Walker."

"Between the lines?"

"Supermarkets kill the Italian way of life. Here, the signora shops the market twice a week, builds relationships—meat from the butcher, vegetables from the grocer. Each sale is personal."

Walker frowned. "And a supermarket?"

"Aisles of convenience. No emotion. No humanity. Just control dressed up as modernity."

"What are you saying?"

Leslie chose an upholstered armchair. Leslie's voice softened. "It's about control, Walker. What better way to alter and influence Italians who have known deprivation during the war. Introduce the idea of a supermarket into the culture because it says, be American, become like us, while we keep our foot close to your throat."

"Close to your throat?"

"As opposed to on it," she said, her voice softer now.

Walker lifted the paper off the bed. "You're saying Dulles is behind this."

"No, my money is on his pet Angleton. Know the name?"

"From Jack, yes, but I've not had the pleasure of meeting the man. Why?"

"Consider the new map of Europe. Italy is the only country not divided, and it has a viable Communist party. The logic here is, it's hard to be a

Commie whilst you have a full belly at the same time. Besides, it makes perfect sense for Dulles to give it to Angleton."

"Because he's Catholic," Walker answered.

"A devout Catholic like Clare Boothe Luce, and don't forget that the late Mussolini made Vatican City sovereign, which has significant financial implications. Oh," she said, "the *spinone italiano* is a pointer."

"How is it you can say the name of a dog breed and make it sound so sexy?"

She blushed. Her chin lifted. "What does that paper say?"

He visited the bed. "Don't you worry someone could be listening in on us?"

"Very likely they are, but our discussion isn't anything they don't already know."

Walker picked up the newspaper. "Everybody but me, it seems." He scanned more newsprint before he tossed it onto the bed. She repeated her question. "What did that paper say?"

He answered, "The Seven Sisters control all the oil, and a politician with the Christian Democrats named Enrico Mattei is in favor of natural gas instead of oil."

That smile again. "Connect the dots yet?"

"Seems like Iran isn't the only country of interest that begins with the letter I." Walker crawled across the bed. "Doesn't this dog deserve a treat?"

She kissed him on the lips.

** * **

There was a knock at their door. The rap of one hard and one soft knock seemed appropriate to a speakeasy. Only the good guys were polite enough to announce their presence.

Walker strode across the room and opened the door to a bruiser in a Brioni suit tailored to obscure the muscles and whatever weapons he may have hidden on his person. He held his hat in his hand and introduced himself as Mr. Rossi.

It didn't require a proof, any advance mathematics, or Einstein at the blackboard in Princeton to deduce that Mr. Rossi was an envoy from the station chief in Rome. He stepped in and said in a monotone voice, "Mr. Colby welcomes you to Rome."

"Any message?" Walker asked.

"Two: one for you and one for the lady."

The man was personable and effusive as wet cement. His hair slicked back with beeswax pomade, the executive part bared a white line of scalp, but not much else for personality. He was fresh off the conveyor belt for small talk.

Walker closed the door. "Ladies first."

"The message for her first?" he asked.

"You did say there were two."

"Yeah, and I was hoping to tell her hers in private."

Leslie spoke. "Whatever you have to say you may say it in front of him."

"Are you sure? It's from Norman." He looked to her and, when Leslie didn't budge, at Walker. "Very well then, he said, and I quote, 'Don't bugger it this time.'"

Walker gestured to a chair, "Won't you have a seat?"

Rossi moved with slow, uncertain steps. The sudden act of hospitality had caught him off guard. He sat in the chair at the desk the hotel provided guests for writing letters home. Walker had hoped that he would sit because the irregular floor made the chair uncomfortable and unstable.

The fingers of Rossi's left hand gripped the crown of his fedora. Walker offered their guest a drink, but Rossi refused the hospitality. He said, "You want your message or what?"

"I'm trying to make nice and not rush you," Walker said.

Rossi looked left and right of his feet. "What's with this chair?" He looked up at Walker and grinned. He shifted his weight from left to right in the chair, such that the wood squeaked. "Bum floor makes for a crummy seat, and you standing over me gives you the advantage. Clever and effective."

"And simple," Walker said and asked, "How long have you been with the Company?"

"Since Christ was a corporal. What's it to you?"

"Curious as to why you report to Colby, but deliver a message from MI6?"

"This is a joint venture, so why wouldn't I?" He stood up and pushed the chair back with his heel. He adjusted his tie and checked his cuffs. "Want your message now?" Rossi didn't seem to trouble his head or his matinee hairstyle when it came to dialog. "The message is, enjoy your tea, but don't lose focus over the crumpet." He rose from his seat, put his lid on, and adjusted the brim with a finger. He nodded to Leslie. "No disrespect intended, Miss. I'm only the messenger."

Walker said, "Can you relay a message for me, Mr. Rossi?"

The big man imitated the Sphinx in the desert and stared at Walker.

Walker counted to three to himself, which prompted Rossi to ask, "Is this message for Colby or Norman?"

"Norman. Tell him I'll think of England when I have my tea and crumpet. Was there a message from the station chief, other than his welcome to Rome?"

"Mr. Dulles and his guest request the pleasure of you two as a couple this evening."

He named the bar downstairs and the time.

Still as stone, like she hadn't heard the door at all.

"Hell of a welcome, don't you think?"

She blinked once. "I'm a crumpet?"

Walker didn't answer. Didn't even blink.

"You and Norman have history?"

Chapter Eleven

T he ride amounted to a half-day, a few hours of pilgrimage on the road. Sign after tacky sign, weather-faded metal mounted on stakes along the interstate, appeared at regular intervals like Lucky Strike ads and the *Hit Parade* on the radio.

Sheldon imagined it as an exodus from the heat and hostility of the Tri-State area to the supposed paradise of the Catskills. For Jews weary of slurs, sweat, and subway grime, the Borscht Belt was more than vacation. It was refuge. A whole summer for the wife and kids or a slice of the Borscht Belt for dad on weekends was *shamayim*.

The Nash-Healey purred up the resort's drive, drawing stares. Jack had arranged everything. A last-minute 'cancellation,' a guest list reshuffled. Sheldon's invented surname floated to the top. A VIP from New England, visiting with his niece, provided sufficient cover to avoid questions. Jack believed in the less-said approach. Sheldon was in publishing. Tania kept her real first name but shaved a few years for the Activities Coordinator.

Sheldon spotted staff converging on cars, bellhops at attention.

They'd be disappointed by the contents of the trunk. He wasn't.

The boys were lean and hopeful, seasonal labor who traded sweat equity for tuition. A summer's work at most resorts paid for books, board, and maybe a future. Deals were made. Romances flickered. Families returned year after year like monarchs to Mexico.

Their mark was one of them.

Benjamin Morris didn't sound Jewish, but Jack's file provided a thumbnail biography. The family had changed their name from Moritz. His print shop started in the Lower East Side and now stood on the Upper West, with clients of every faith. The rabbis approved so long as his literature didn't proselytize. The business had branches in Jerusalem and Tehran, and produced posters, calendars, greeting cards, and government pamphlets. What mattered most to the Company was that Morris owned the only two Xerox machines in Iran.

Sheldon stepped out as a valet moved in. A boy with a swimmer's shoulders helped Tania out of the car. A man with a clipboard, in a sweat-darkened jacket, stepped up, smiling like a salesman.

Sheldon gave their name before he was asked. The man slipped him a folded paper with the discretion of a pickpocket. The piece of paper listed Suggested Gratuities, twelve to twenty dollars per staffer, per week.

He launched into his spiel of three meals daily: a modest breakfast, dairy for lunch, meat for dinner, and all the food was All-you-can-eat. For Tania's benefit, he added: "Girls watch their figures, of course." He smiled. "But you'd see Elijah at your table before worrying about yours, dear."

Tania gave him a tight smile. Sheldon said nothing. He could've done without the sight of the melted pomade that trickled down the back of the man's neck.

They were handed keys to a His-and-Her suite, nicer than most. The man explained the talent show—a tradition. Kids practiced weeks in advance.

"Does the little lady have any special skills?" he asked.

Tania took off her sunglasses. She squinted. "Why?"

"There's a lottery for acts. If your name comes up, you'd better be ready. There's a cash prize. And a trophy." He grinned like it was his first time delivering the line. It wasn't. He leaned in close. "A dish like you will have the boys in a tizzy all summer."

"I'll be merciful," she said.

He smirked. "A girl needs more than looks. Gotta have a talent. What do you say, dear?"

Tania put on her sunglasses. "I'm sure I'll find one before I leave."

He glanced at Sheldon. "Modest, isn't she?"

Sheldon met his eyes. "And modesty can kill."

Chapter Twelve

The first full day exhausted him. Sheldon found a quiet spot with a small glass and his bottle of Springback Single Malt Scotch whisky—brought from Boston, a parting choice from Jack's collection. They'd had their differences, not least of which was that Jack insisted on spelling whisky with an e.

He found a lonesome pier that jutted out into the lake. Cicadas droned. A summer breeze swept in from the east while the sun died in the west. Clouds became shadows against a screen of orange and red. Now and then, fireflies blinked like faulty signals.

Nature mourned without knowing why.

He unfolded one of the deck chairs and sat. Poured. Counted to four. Stared at the lake, the glass still in his hand.

As the last light faded, the water turned ominous.

Still, but not at peace.

Instinct stirred. Someone behind him.

He turned. Tania.

He raised his chin in acknowledgment but said nothing.

She didn't ask. Just pulled a chair over and sat.

The scent of aged wood mingled uneasily with the plastic of the cushion. Tania smelled of moss and citrus—her usual Tweed by Lenthéric, a bottle she'd picked up in London.

They sat in silence for a few minutes.

Sheldon waited. In his experience, women were the ones who crossed the silence. Men folded it away like a stubborn shirt.

She didn't disappoint.

"This place isn't all latkes, love, and laughter for you, is it?"

He took a sip. "No, it is not."

He offered her the glass, but she waved it off. Not because of her age—she'd done worse than drink in Europe.

"So what is the elephant in the room? That's the expression, right?

"The elephant is that I feel like a stranger among my own people."

"You do keep to yourself. You don't go to Temple," she said. "Not a criticism."

"A valid observation. There's no solace in faith for me. Not after what happened." He shook his head. "I don't understand how Hashem could allow evil in the world."

Tania wasn't religious, but she knew better than to say "God" like Gentiles did. Jews said Hashem, 'the Name,' out of reverence. Even Yahweh was written without vowels. Never spoken aloud.

A firefly blinked and vanished.

The silence accepted it.

"I'm not a theologian, Uncle Shelly, so I can't offer you an explanation."

"These people here," he said, with a glance over his shoulder, as if tossing salt, "they didn't see it. Not with their own eyes. They lost relatives, yes—but not one of them saw the terror."

"You don't know that."

She reached for the glass. Swirled it gently, watching it catch the last light.

"I'm certain some here fled for their lives. Or left people behind. Or struggle every day with how to tell their children. Pain isn't a single path."

"You don't sense the difference?" he asked.

"Difference in what?"

"The ones who grew up here—and those who didn't."

She took a sip, small and deliberate. No flinch. No scowl. Just a taste and a thought.

"An ocean separates the two. Language, culture... distance. We're survivors. It marks you. You know that. People here—once they see the numbers on your arm—they don't know what to do. Is what's upsetting you that you have to leverage that to help Jack?"

"No," he said. He didn't look at her.

Didn't want her to see it.

Staring at the water, he had the urge to run screaming into the dark until the lake silenced him.

"Some of them here might be survivors too," she said.

He nodded slowly. "I know. But not everyone wears it on the outside. I do. That's the difference."

"You make it sound like anthropology."

"It is," he said. "You read Margaret Mead. Remind me again what she said."

She told him Mead believed civilization began with the discovery of a healed femur—proof that someone stayed with the injured long enough for them to recover. Sheldon had disagreed with her at the time. Mead called it civilization. He called it compassion.

Both agreed: kindness isn't logical. It's a decision. Stay so others may live.

"I don't know much about your religion beyond what I've read. So this is going to sound reductive, possibly offensive. But I'd say American Jews are more vocal." She held up a hand. "And yes, I know I'm an inch away from a stereotype. But no American, Jew or not, understands what it's like to live under secret police. To wonder if your neighbor will turn you in. Americans fret about Communists like it's a movie plot."

"They should meet the Stasi," Sheldon said, a grin as he took a sip.

Silence settled.

At thirteen, when they met, all signs pointed to atheism at home. She'd told Sheldon once that Christianity obsessed over the next world at the expense of this one. In her mind, it disrespected the present.

It deferred justice. Deferred joy.

She'd fought with nuns who taught that Judaism was the first monotheism.

"Zoroastrianism came first," she told them. It had been founded in Iran.

Yahweh, she told them, was once one god among many—a desert warlord.

The Israelites had slaughtered their cousins.

"The Old Testament," she said in her infamous class presentation, "is a record of tribal wars."

Sheldon might have dismissed it as bravado, adolescent revolt, but he understood her.

Stalin had murdered her father. She had fled to Budapest. Learned Hungarian. Spoke French like an aristocrat. German came later—or perhaps it claimed her.

Like him, she had killed the people who harmed her.

She took another sip of the whisky.

No flinch. No wincing. Just control.

She understood pain that would break most men.

Wore it like an extra layer of skin.

And she considered most men weak.

Chapter Thirteen

The resort was alive with activities from sunrise to sunset, and they learned that there were four meals served instead of three because their host had neglected to mention the midnight meal. The captain of the dining hall introduced Sheldon and Tania to their table—the one they'd keep for the duration.

Sheldon read the faces around the table during the introductions. They were replacing a family unable to attend this holiday season. The smiles were tight and polite, but their eyes said that he and Tania were usurpers of chairs that belonged to their friends. Two additional chairs implied there were children among the absent party.

At lunch and dinner on that first day, the conversations were the usual and expected superficial kind—car rides, where Sheldon and Tania hailed from—before drifting into banalities about Boston, colonial history, and other New England stereotypes, seasonal and otherwise. The table brimmed with an abundance of plate after plate of food until the white tablecloth was barely visible. By the time coffee arrived, everyone was waiting for dessert, and the tenor of the conversation drifted to the tribulations Jews faced in Beantown—doctors with legitimate licenses unable to practice until they formed Beth Israel Hospital. It was said that with time and some tolerance, Jewish neighborhoods spread from East Boston to Dorchester and Roxbury. A couple among the party, the Feldmans, who had lived in Boston's West End before moving to Manhattan, narrated most of the commentary.

The survey of history ended when all eyes in the room focused on a parade of waiters who wheeled in a caravan of carts and cloches for a symphonic, theatrical serving of flambéed cherries jubilee. The elderly lady next to Sheldon informed him that evening there would be an arsonist's delight. She said that he should expect Crêpes Suzette, Bananas Foster, Crêpes Mylene, and her personal favorite, Omelette Vallée d'Auge. She added that diners had recently petitioned for the addition of Mangos Diablo and Pêches Louis.

While they watched the waiters make the dessert with the precision of the Rockettes at Radio City Music Hall, Sheldon ignored the orchestral eruption of blue flames, the sound of the audience's reaction. He wondered whether Jack had left it to him to find Ben Morris. Sheldon had hoped that Jack would have saved him time and placed him at the same table. He concluded that his room was adjacent—or in close proximity—to Ben and his family's.

Tania's experience of the first day and night differed from Sheldon's.

She identified three cliques of girls in the ecosystem: Broads, Dames, and Ladies. The noir taxonomy pleased her.

She watched them move and commiserate in groups, often at scheduled activities or, like this evening, congregate in the back of the room. Tania couldn't help but think how dull they all were. They moved with the mechanical grace of wind-up dolls.

Tania noticed the boys, too, and found them simple. She wondered how they managed to dress themselves without Mother's help. She accepted the scene before her as both sociological and biological. Both genders did their version of the preen and strut, the display of what they had to offer a prospective mate. It was all a preparatory class for Marriage, Mortgage, and Maternity.

She sat next to one of the vacant chairs. She, too, felt eyes on her and, when nobody spoke to her, assumed that it was because they knew she was not Jewish. Or maybe they didn't care. They probably wouldn't even notice if she vanished. She anticipated gossip around her presence and her connection to Sheldon, even though he had introduced her as his niece.

She ate in silence and observed the people around her table. Walter Moskowitz, across from her, chided his wife on what she ate and how much, and stole food off her plate with his fork. His wife Miriam translated the same misery to her daughter next to her, reminding her that boys did not go for zaftig or too much chutzpah. What food she lost to the husband, the mother regained through theft from her child.

Tania tried not to look embarrassed in front of the girl when their eyes met over the forest of dishes and glasses. Awkward. Tania focused on her entrée, her fork not interested in the chicken, the eternal choice of chefs for large crowds. As her tines teased the meat, she remembered that Sheldon had explained to her that Jews adhered to Kashrut, or dietary laws. The difference between a kosher and a regular chicken was that the bird had to be killed a certain way and by a trained expert called a *shochet*. Tania liked the sharp and lethal sound of the word. The name for the specialist would become code between them for an assassin.

Tania felt a hand pull on her sleeve. She looked and found a young girl of ten sitting in the chair. The child leaned forward to say something privately. Tania tilted her ear to the girl's lips and heard,

"That's not very nice of that man over there to take food off the lady's dish."

Tania didn't bother to look—she knew the child was talking about Walter Moskowitz.

"No, it's not nice," she said, "especially when there's plenty of food on the table."

"What would you do if your boyfriend or husband did that to you?"

Tania said, "I would never be with someone like that," but what she wanted to say was that she would put either a fork or a knife through his hand.

"What's your name?"

"Ruth. Can I ask you another question?" The girl touched a button on Tania's blouse. "Why aren't the buttons on your shirt on the right and not on the left? Are you left-handed?"

Tania glanced down at her blouse.

"If you must know, this blouse is from Europe, and the buttons are on the opposite side because there was a time when a lady had a servant help her dress. The buttons are there to help the maid. You're very observant, Ruth. You ought to be a writer or a detective."

"Mother said ladies don't write crime stories."

Tania almost bit her tongue. She asked her new friend, "Have a library card, Ruth?"

The child nodded enthusiastically.

She was thinking she'd burn the house down with Mother inside, but said instead, "Then you have all you need to set the world on fire."

They would've talked more, but the lights dimmed twice to signal that the evening's entertainment was about to start. A master of ceremonies reminded the crowd that the Borscht Belt was home to many upcoming and famous comedians. Tania had heard that many entertainers in Las Vegas had honed their craft, whether it was skits or songs, here in the Borscht Belt.

She braced herself.

The first comedian stepped up. He opened with wordplay: 'jus' and Jews, and moved on.

"What's the difference between a Rottweiler and a Jewish mother?"

A deliberate pause for the punchline.

"At some point, the Rottweiler will let go."

Tania groaned, knowing variety acts awaited her the rest of the evening, and wished vaudeville were dead. Comedians, like the young man on stage, were there to test their material on the audience at the resort and some of the nearby bungalow colonies. She anticipated the sounds of Big Band music. It wasn't the tunes 'kids' listened to these days, but the adults considered it clean and as kosher as the food served in the Jewish Alps.

A telltale symbol of nostalgia in the room was the Style H Wurlitzer organ from the days of Prohibition. The only act missing was that of Jack 'Legs Diamond' Moran, the notorious bootlegger who hid out in the Catskills to burst onstage and imitate a Jewish James Cagney, who, Tania heard from Walker, was fluent in Yiddish from a childhood spent in Manhattan's Lower East Side. She had overheard someone say that Louis Armstrong had been unofficially adopted by a Jewish couple named Karnofsky. Ambassador Satch wore a Star of David as gratitude for the couple's generosity and support.

"Excuse me," a voice said, and Tania looked up. Before her stood a balding, bulbous, beetle-browed man with a hula-hoop for a belly and midsection, a thin leather belt holding his pants above white socks in dull black shoes. A necktie, as an afterthought, hung far north of his navel.

"I see you met my daughter Ruth. My name is Benjamin Morris."

Tania stood up; she towered over the man.

"A pleasure to meet you, Mr. Morris."

"Benjamin, please," he said, pronouncing the name in Hebrew.

Tania noted the difference in pronunciation since she was accustomed to its German version. She felt Sheldon rise behind her when he heard the man announce himself. Two small boys in suits and ties ran between them.

Morris said, "It ought to be against the law for boys under the age of eighteen to have to wear a tie in public." He stepped closer to Sheldon and Tania and whispered,

"Mind if we step away from the table and talk?"

The two men, Tania, and young Ruth stepped away.

"Sorry about that," Ben Morris said. "It's just that Moskowitz is a real pain in the tuchus."

Tania responded, "I'd rather thought him a schmuck for the way he treats his wife."

"Yes," the stout man said, and glanced over at Sheldon, "I like this one; she's feisty."

"You don't know the half of it, but she's a good egg," Sheldon said and introduced himself as Tania's uncle.

"Unlike most men, I appreciate candor in a woman," the man said, somewhat perplexed when he noticed Ruth counting on her fingers. "What are you doing, sweetheart?"

In wide-eyed innocence, Ruth said, "Trying to figure out their age difference?"

Ben Morris, hands on his daughter's shoulders now, apologized.

"Please forgive her. She doesn't understand what is and isn't polite conversation."

As he spoke, a young woman, a few years shy of Tania's eighteenth year, floated in behind him.

She said softly, "Abi." An affectionate word for father.

Ben seemed embarrassed.

"How could I forget? This is my other daughter, Judith. Another reason why I chose to stay away from the table. I don't need that lecherous toad leering at my girls. Have you seen him in action?"

"Only with food," Sheldon said. "Tania and I arrived today."

"Give it time, and you'll see the man is a real *chazer*, and proof that a pig is not the only other white meat."

Sheldon nodded in understanding. Ben asked Sheldon where he was from and what he did for a living. Sheldon lied; he said that he was a publisher. Ben complimented Sheldon on his impeccable clothes, and Sheldon replied that in another life he'd been a tailor.

Ben lifted his arms.

"I wish I knew you in that other life. I'd call upon your skills in the sartorial arts to make me less of an eyesore in public."

Judith, tall and buxom, smiled and eyed the floor, almost painfully embarrassed to hear about Moskowitz or her father's self-deprecating remarks about his appearance. While her papa chatted with Sheldon, Tania stepped forward, took Judith by the hand, and escorted her away to a nearby window.

"Let the men talk while we get to know each other, Judith."

"Thank you. You are so kind, and please call me Judy."

"I don't mean to sound presumptuous, but you don't seem happy here."

Judith avoided direct eye contact, but Tania saw her new acquaintance's eyes drift to someone—or to something—behind her, and then down again. Tania checked the glass behind Judy and saw the reflection of a gaggle of girls flit by and disappear out of sight.

Walking stereotypes.

"Let me guess—the local mavens?"

"Not the first word beginning with the letter M that I would've picked, but, yes, they're the local divas."

"And the other word that begins with M?" Tania asked.

"It's Yiddish for witch."

Tania glanced over her shoulder and found the group in the crowded room.

"Oh, you mean they're bitches." Tania faced Judy. "Where's your mom?"

"In the city. With her new boyfriend."

The 'city' was what everyone in the Tri-state area called Manhattan.

"Boyfriend?"

"My parents are headed for divorce court, which is why Papa has ballooned into J. Wellington Wimpy, except he eats more than hamburgers and owes everyone, including Popeye, money."

"That bad?" Tania asked.

"Divorce or the money? It doesn't matter since both are costing him his health. Although Papa hopes to land a major deal to avoid the poorhouse—if not for the politicians and one anti-Semite in particular. Sorry, I talk so much, and I wear my heart on my sleeve. I shouldn't burden you. Nobody likes a complainer. People prefer a lighthouse to a lifeboat."

Tania looked over her shoulder—not at the troublesome pack of girls who liked to sharpen their claws and teeth—but at Sheldon and Ben Morris, in rapt conversation. Tania turned her attention back to her new friend and squeezed Judy's hand.

She squeezed it and said, "You'll find out that I'm not most people."

Chapter Fourteen

At six o'clock, Walker stepped outside for some air before heading to the bar for aperitifs. Leslie said she'd meet him there in a few minutes. She reminded him that Italians called the pre-meal drink *aperitivo*. She added a touch of etymology, explaining that their word for cocktail came from the Latin *aperire*, meaning 'to open,' and eventually came to mean 'to open the stomach before dining'—a gruesome image he could have done without, especially since they were about to meet Dulles plus one.

He expressed surprise that Clare Boothe Luce, Ambassador to Italy, would be seen in public with the Company's Director. Leslie shrugged. "Why not? The embassy is right there." She didn't bother to point, but she did consult him on two dress options. He chose the one she held against her, not the one she was wearing.

"Whichever you pick," he said, "please keep your accent straight. You tend to slip between British and American English, depending on who's in the room."

"You're in a mood," she said, but the comment didn't seem to land the way she intended.

* * *

An impromptu thunderstorm had come and gone. Rain fell in thick sheets, drumming the roof of the Excelsior and lashing the windows. The air was now charged. He smelled ozone—sharp, metallic, electric. He had been a different man when they first arrived, but here, in this city that carried scars of war, he couldn't tell what had changed. It wasn't just the rain.

Outside, an Italian approached and pantomimed a request for a cigarette, but Walker shrugged. He was perhaps the only American in all of Rome who didn't smoke. The man likely hoped for a Camel. Anything American carried status. Europe, fresh with optimism and eager to forget the war, was alive with distractions. Boys slicked their hair into pompadours, girls swooned over actors and singers. The air was thick with Brylcreem, and knees buckled.

He hadn't asked Leslie about the boy at the train station or dug deeper about Norman Darbyshire. He suspected there was a story. Still, he said nothing. The silence between them had grown comfortable in its discomfort.

Italy remained a wounded phoenix. The drive from Ciampino to the hotel provided ample proof. Ironically, the airport's callsign was CIA.

The streets were alive with vendors selling apples, *grattachecca*, and pizza curbside. Their driver, a Roman who spoke fluent English, recommended the Jewish ghetto for *abbacchio amatriciana*. He warned them about thieves on bicycles and con artists near the Spanish Steps and the Trevi Fountain. He glanced at Leslie in the rearview mirror and cautioned her to expect catcalls and pinches. Walker grinned, doubting anyone would try to grope Leslie twice.

Pickpockets, the driver warned, were legion. The *pizzardoni*, local police directing traffic in lieu of lights, wouldn't bother with tourists' complaints.

Rome bore her scars. Bullet-pocked walls. Empty blocks where bombs had leveled buildings. Political posters plastered every surface. The Marshall Plan was in full swing, rebuilding a continent. But here, in the city's bones, the past could not be erased. While Europe healed, back home in the States, Jack's daughter Elizabeth and girls like her drank milkshakes at soda counters, waiting for a boy in Study Hall to ask them out.

Walker checked his watch. Time. The doorman opened the door.

* * *

Dulles was already seated, his presence as if conjured. A red drink, bitter and carbonated, sat untouched before him. A plate of chips, nuts, and olives lay undisturbed.

Walker spied the drink and thought: Communism or blood. Either suited the man. Everything about Dulles was symbolic or subtext. Churchill had once said, "The only bull I know who carries his china closet with him."

"A Negroni, please."

The waiter nodded and moved off. Behind the bar, a faint radio played. Walker scanned the room—entrances, exits, mirrors. He turned his back to Dulles only because the bar's mirrored glass gave him a full view. No angle unobserved.

Drink in hand, he turned back. Dulles rose for the handshake—as all men do, or should.

Dulles inquired after Leslie. Walker said she'd arrive soon.

"The ambassador will be here any moment," Dulles confirmed.

Leslie entered in a pale tangerine sweater, doeskin pants, a loosely tied cravat. She offered Dulles both hands, leaned in for two air kisses, French-style. Walker had learned the French called it *la bise*. He preferred the unambiguous, universal, and asexual handshake.

Dulles pulled out her chair.

The bartender arrived, and without his asking, Leslie ordered a spritz with Prosecco.

Almost on cue, Clare Boothe Luce walked in—blonde, stylish, composed, a Dior suit and the air of someone who had just stepped off a stage. She greeted Dulles and Walker in the European style, and complimented Leslie on her colors.

"You look lovely, darling. It's as if you knew that peach is my favorite color."

"I might've intercepted intelligence to that effect."

Luce called everyone 'darling.'

Leslie, Walker realized, had dressed down, as in not to compete. Luce was a master tactician. She kept her smile like the hat on her head: fixed, precise, a choice. She'd been to the Front, behind desks, and left more than one general in her wake. Playwright, socialite, intellectual.

Walker wondered what she saw in Dulles. Unless Bonaparte was right: power is the greatest aphrodisiac.

Leslie admired two of Luce's quotes:

'Simplicity is the ultimate sophistication,' and 'Nature abhors a virgin—a frozen asset.'

The latter made Walker uneasy.

Clare disliked being told she had a 'masculine mind.' Her answer was to say, 'Thought has no sex. One either thinks, or one does not.' She'd opposed the Wayward Wives Bill and argued that if a soldier cheated overseas, his wife's benefits should double.

They sat. Clare ordered a large Scotch.

"A bad day?" Dulles asked.

"Work. Endless work."

"Not your usual style."

She glanced at Leslie. "He means well. My first husband was an angel sober, a demon drunk. After my daughter's accident, I nearly turned to the bottle. Then I found the cure, and a miraculous analyst. What was his name?"

"Ormond, in London. He called the cure a psychedelic."

Clare took a slow sip. "LSD."

Leslie raised her glass. "My condolences on your loss. To happier memories."

Clare lifted her own. "To Ann. And to your success in Rome, God willing."

Dulles clinked last. Then he offered a précis of their careers. When he mentioned Dachau, Leslie squeezed Walker's thigh under the table.

He said little but enough. Clare had seen Buchenwald's aftermath. She knew.

Then came the reason for the meeting from Dulles. They would deliver a personal message to Reinhard Gehlen. Neither Leslie nor Walker blinked.

Clare drank her whisky. Then, as if decoding Dulles:

"Gehlen needs reminding. His organization isn't to compete with the Company. Germany and Eastern Europe only. Not Italy. Questions?"

Walker looked at Leslie, then answered. "What's the message?"

"We're using another bank."

"He'll understand what that means?"

Dulles nodded. "The seed money for Tehran won't come from Switzerland. The Company has new financing. Here. In Rome."

Walker tilted his glass. "And how will he take that?"

Dulles gave a slight smile. "No harm will befall the heralds, if that's your concern."

"None," Leslie said. "I understand."

"You understand?"

"*Miserando atque eligendo*," Clare said, with a glint of something else in her eyes.

Dulles raised his glass. "You do understand."

"Let's enjoy our drinks," the ambassador said.

They talked of home. Clare told stories—how she'd stormed Condé Nast's office, demanded a job, and stayed until he hired her. How she wrote the play *The Women* in three days and paid for it with a lifetime of envy from other writers.

Whether truth or not, she told stories well.

She revealed she was brokering peace between Italy and Yugoslavia. Tito would soon break with Moscow, she claimed. Diplomacy was a mask—every side needed to save face.

Walker was struck by her voice. Not Mid-Atlantic. Not quite Connecticut. A dialect from nowhere and everywhere.

She rose. "I must tend to papers at the Villa," she said, then touched Dulles's shoulder. "Do look into that matter, Allen. I insist."

After she left, Leslie asked, "Is everything okay?"

"She believes someone's poisoning her."

"Poisoning her?"

"She's not prone to paranoia. But I'll have it looked into."

Dulles finished his drink and stood. "Expect an address in Lugano. *Buona notte*."

The chips, nuts, and olives remained untouched.

Walker had paced his Negroni. Leslie had noticed. They sat in silence. Clare had left an impression. Walker asked, "I'm rusty on my Latin."

"The calling of St. Matthew. He was a tax collector, and that was her way of saying the money is coming from the Church. She has interesting eyes, doesn't she?" Leslie said.

"She does."

"More blue or green?"

"Aquamarine."

"Aquamarine," she repeated.

He sensed her watching him. "No reaction to Germany?"

"Nope. Plane, train, automobile. All the same."

"Finish your drink, Walker."

He didn't like the command in her tone, almost testing him. "I was thinking."

"Now we're in trouble," she smiled. "A lira for your thoughts."

He sipped. "We're to tell a former Nazi—no Nazi money."

"Correct."

"Because it's coming from Vatican City?"

"Thanks to Mussolini. Sovereign territory, and the money isn't traceable."

"Same could be said of Switzerland."

"Yes. But this way, we gain a new ally."

He drained his Negroni. "A Nazi or the Church. And the lady ambassador herself as midwife. Thoughts?"

"She can stand on her own. She has her own money, which means the boys don't own or control her. She's dangerous in all the right ways." Her eyes went cold.

He waited.

"She has a middle name they forget."

"Boothe. So?"

"She added the 'e.' But there's still an assassin in the family."

Chapter Fifteen

Tania sat on a bench atop a small hill, watching a group of women and girls—mothers and daughters, she presumed—do morning calisthenics. They moved like recruits in Basic Training, puffing and straining to impress the instructor. Clad in a snug black singlet, he wore a nickel-plated whistle and barked orders, "Sets and reps, ladies. Sets and reps."

Tania watched as his victims of either fitness or lust stole furtive glances at their PE instructor, a kosher Jack LaLanne, brought to life in the Catskills from some Hollywood studio.

In the distance, a game of badminton played out, with what sounded like mild Yiddish curses punctuating missed swings at the birdie. Through her green lenses, Tania surveyed the lake below. A fleet of canoes and paddle boats drifted like windless sails. The sun, relentless, kept its promise to climb higher, delivering a punishing day. No clouds, just the expanse of gorgeous, pitiless blue.

"Morning," came a voice behind her.

Tania turned to see Ruth. The young girl asked if she could sit. Tania nodded and asked how she'd slept, whether breakfast had been good. Ruth stuck out her tongue in response.

"Good thing you're not Jewish. You've been spared the horror of our cuisine."

Tania smiled. "Oh, I don't know. I've heard you have wonderful soups—Jewish penicillin—and I've been to Katz's for pastrami. It can't be all bad."

"You can't eat that every day. Might as well have a cigarette for breakfast."

"Some people do," Tania said. "How come you're not in some activity, or is it too early?"

"I'm not what you'd call athletic." Ruth flexed her bicep like Rosie the Riveter.

"I think the idea is to have fun."

"Speak for yourself. What's your excuse?"

"You've heard the expression 'the only Jew in the room'?"

Ruth squinted and held her hand up—not to salute, but to block the glare. "My people invented the saying. What of it?"

Tania leaned forward. "I'm the only Gentile in the room."

"Feeling all the love, are you?"

"Yep," Tania said, and smacked her lips for emphasis. She turned sideways on the bench. "Where is your sister Judith?"

Ruth looked over her shoulder and back again. "Inside with Papa. They were arguing."

"Arguing about what, if I may ask?"

"Judy wants to try out roller-skating class."

"And your father is not a fan?"

"He says it's what coloreds do."

Tania went to say something, hesitated. "Coloreds?"

"Black people. Roller skating is their thing. I'm surprised you didn't know."

Tania smiled, though it was thin. "Why would I?"

"Roller skating is popular in Boston."

"Is it? I must've missed that." Tania paused. "So what's Papa's objection?"

Ruth shot her a look that suggested the question didn't deserve an answer. But Tania held her gaze, waiting.

Ruth sighed. "He says derby girls fight. Like animals."

"Have you tried it yourself?"

"It was sweaty and messy, and some girl grabbed me to stop from falling."

Judith approached and greeted them. Ruth fell silent.

"I should go," Ruth mumbled and turned to leave.

"You don't have to," Judith said.

"It's okay. This one needs company. She's lonely."

Judith glanced at Tania. "Lonely? I don't understand. I saw Sheldon just a moment ago."

"Only Gentile in the Room Syndrome," Ruth whispered.

Tania said, "I don't think it's contagious." She removed her Vuranet sunglasses. "Here. Wear these before the glare gives you a headache."

Ruth hesitated. "They're cool. I'll take care of them, but what about you?"

"I've got Ray-Bans as backup."

They watched Ruth go.

"That was kind of you," Judith said. "I saw you sitting here alone. Thought you were deep in thought, or am I wrong?"

"You saw me?"

"From the dining room. Papa's table."

"I didn't think I was visible."

"You were," Judith said, "and it looked like you were off somewhere in your head."

"I was," Tania said. "Seeing the lake, the boats, reminded me of a trip a long time ago. With my father. We went to Wannsee, outside of Berlin. Rowboats, the smell of water, birds. I was about Ruth's age, maybe younger. It's all a blur, but a pleasant one."

"With your papa?"

"*Ja, mit meinem geliebten Vater.*" Tania froze. The words slipped out before she could stop them, lingering in the air like a misplayed note.

She recovered quickly. "Yes, with my beloved father. Sorry."

"Sounds like a lovely memory. I assume you lost him."

Tania nodded. "To Stalin's henchmen."

Judith sighed. "It was either Hitler or Stalin."

Tania gave a dry laugh. "The Italians have a saying. Between the hammer and the anvil. I'd say, Stalin swung the sickle." She slapped her knee, suddenly self-conscious. "I also remember this boy I saw at the lake. My first crush, I guess. Blond hair like straw. Blue eyes like lace agate. A poster boy for Aryan superiority. For all I know, he was in the Hitler Youth."

"Hitler Youth?"

Tania nodded. "Think of the Boy Scouts, if they had swastikas. I'm sorry I brought it up."

"Why sorry?" Judith's forehead creased.

"Anything German is sensitive."

"It is to my father's generation. I get it. But I can't hate someone for being German. Think about the president. Eisenhower? You can't get more German than that."

Judith pinched the material on Tania's shoulder. "Did you talk to this boy at the lake?"

"No, I didn't, Judy. He was a silly crush."

Chapter Sixteen

ania heard the voice behind her, turned her head, and didn't need to use her hand as a visor against the sun's glare because the rotund body of Benjamin Morris provided a temporary solar eclipse.

"You should've kept the sunglasses instead of giving them to Ruth. I'll make sure she returns them to you."

"She can keep them, Mr. Morris. They were a gift."

"Thank you. I told you to call me Ben, and I meant it. I insist, please. Anything but Mr. Morris. I'm trying to forget I'm on the precipice of middle age, and a divorce."

"I'd tease you and suggest you see an analyst, but it looks like you've got self-flagellation under control."

"Analysis?" He looked at her with a wry smile. "Couldn't afford it. I'm an impossible case. At least Catholics have a saint for hopeless causes."

Tania squeezed his thigh. "Nothing a good cilice or a short-whip couldn't cure."

He smiled. "We Jews have a sauna and a *venik*. Pain and perspiration, as our own sacraments. Impressive vocabulary."

Most people didn't know what a cilice was—an undergarment of penance and pain—or the *venik*, the fragrant bundle of birch or eucalyptus used as a sauna whisk. Tania knew the former from her time with nuns in Boston, the latter from her father's Russian roots. The nun with the masculine name who taught Latin had said the sauna where they opened the veins was a place for a final act of atonement for wayward Romans. The *venik platza*, a Slavic remedy for skin and nerves.

Ben sighed. "Nothing is more unattractive than a self-pitying walrus of a man. I don't have much going for me, so I need all the help I can get to stay afloat in this great bathtub we call life. Got any survival tips for the marginally afloat?"

"All we can do is try. Sink, swim, or tread water, Benny."

His face lit up at the sound of his first name, and that she used a diminutive. "Thank you." He waved a finger. "Kindness and compassion should not go unnoticed. My apologies if I kvetch, but I do what I can to plotz through life. I feel like I'm drowning in a teaspoon. Any wisdom from the frontlines of youth?"

"A Russian proverb comes to mind," Tania said. "It translates into English as, 'Feel the fear and do it anyway.' You'll survive your troubles, even if it feels like you won't."

"You know Russian. Impressed again." He nodded. "My people have perfected the art of self-deprecation. It's really a strategy—make yourself small in front of predators. If they can't see you, they can't eat or shoot you. What do you say to that?"

Tania cocked her head. "Doesn't change the fact there are predators."

He raised an eyebrow. "Men forget that women meet them early. It's always something or someone." His hand moved across an invisible table. "The newsmen warn us about Communists, degenerate music, juvenile delinquency."

Tania put a hand to her mouth, laughing softly.

"Did I say something funny?"

"I found the phrase 'degenerate music' amusing. The Nazis said the same about Chagall, Picasso, and Schiele. All diseased, grotesque, perverse. Every generation finds a new menace. I'm sure your parents objected to jazz and the Charleston."

Ben nodded. "I can see it now."

"See what?"

"Your future husband. He'll have his hands full. Sheldon said you've done well in your studies, but you lack direction."

"Direction? I can see him saying that."

"'Outspoken' was the word he used."

She examined a hangnail. "Did he mention that he's a Russian Jew?"

He did. And mentioned the name of his village. What happened there. Rather depressing. I hope you have a proverb for levity."

Tania said something foreign.

He crossed his arms, waiting.

"I'll prescribe a proverb, since you can't afford psychoanalysis. Want it straight?"

"By all means."

"A bad dancer blames his testicles."

He winced, then smiled. "Quite the vivid image. Point taken: no excuses."

They sat in silence for a minute, watching the second wave of fitness enthusiasts begin their session. The instructor in the snug singlet yelled. Waiters delivered refreshments, young men unfolded beach chairs, and umbrellas bloomed like colorful mushrooms under the unforgiving sun.

"I saw you talking to Judy," he said. His tone changed.

Tania responded in kind. "And you spent most of your morning with my uncle."

"Let's hope the Moskowitzes don't poison the table against him. Make no mistake about it—it is their table. Miriam Moskowitz is a known terror and a registered autocrat. Stalin and Tito could have taken lessons from her."

He leaned closer, whispering. "No matter how polished the silverware is, she'll send it back. It's as if she lives for this season so she can inflict pain."

He cataloged her crimes. Every resort in the Catskills served food in massive quantities, bought in bulk, delivered weekly. It wasn't gourmet, but it was decent. Miriam the Marauder would read the menus and insist on something custom. She put the d in diva—and capitalized it. Even though the staff took notes each season, she'd change her request yearly.

This summer's torment? Shirred eggs.

She must've spent the year researching culinary agonies. Shirred eggs were either baked in cream in a flat-bottom dish or tortured on the stovetop.

"Most people are happy with scrambled, soft, or hard-boiled. Some get adventurous, order Eggs Benedict, a frittata, a poached egg. But not her.

This is the year of the tyrannical shirred egg à la Moskowitz. Count yourself lucky if you haven't witnessed the horror."

"I saw her eat. The family spectacle was enough."

Ben gave a nod. "We all have our troubles. You've heard mine. What ails you?"

Tania raised an eyebrow. "You want a proper kvetch?"

"This is a proper kvetch. A time-honored tradition."

"If I had a complaint, I'd say I'm an outsider here. Your daughters soften the ice, but it's ironic for a people demonized through history, you sure know how to shun. Not to conjure Miriam, but I can suck the egg for the rest of the summer. I've survived worse."

"I gathered that, from talking to your uncle. But I can explain it."

"Explain what?"

"Why they treat you like a pariah. They'll make sure you don't forget what you are. Do you know what a *shiksa* is?"

"I think so." She crossed a leg. A breeze made her shiver. "It means I'm unwanted. Unwelcome. An abomination in their eyes. I threaten their existence. Am I accurate?"

He unfolded his arms.

"Accurate as lightning."

Chapter Seventeen

Sheldon would've preferred his car to the 1949 Ford Custom that Benjamin Morris drove. The short, balding, and thick-legged man with the face of a Pekingese insisted on his vehicle for the road trip. Ben called it 'The Shoebox' for a reason. The automobile was flat, broad, a slab of steel.

Ben's color choice didn't help. Birch Gray made it look more like a floating casket than a car. The vehicle shuddered to a stop in front of Sheldon, and the bellhop seemed relieved that Sheldon himself reached for the door handle.

Sheldon, who worked in colors for his clients, always recommended a classic palette: dark blue or silver for fall and winter, tan or olive for spring and summer. Black was eternal, both for suits and cars.

He slid into the passenger seat while Ben drove through the sylvan landscape. Ben made small talk, mentioning how the great state of New York was busy building the Thruway to connect the Hudson Valley to Manhattan. The massive project, he said, would wake small towns like Rip Van Winkle from their slumber and usher them into the twentieth century.

About halfway through their odyssey, Ben announced, "I have to tinkle," and pulled into a diner parking lot.

"I was last in line when God handed out bladders. Mine's the size of a thimble."

Polite to a fault, Sheldon nodded. "No need to worry. I could use a refreshment myself."

While Sheldon waited, he rotated the selector on the tabletop jukebox and scanned the song list. Ben had yet to order a drink, so Sheldon requested iced water and a slice of cobbler. The waitress delivered everything in one precise motion, like she was handling steins at Oktoberfest.

Ben slid into the booth and gave Sheldon a grateful nod as he reached for his water. His fingers drummed the surface of the turquoise sea-foam Formica. He peeled the paper off his straw and said, "How come you didn't tell me?"

"Tell you what?"

"That you were a survivor."

Sheldon didn't look up. "Didn't see the need to bring it up."

"You must've seen how people reacted last night when they saw the numbers on your arm."

Sheldon lied. "That wasn't my intention."

"I know we haven't known each other long, but I have to ask you a question."

Sheldon swallowed. "What was it like?"

Ben nodded.

"Hell on earth," Sheldon answered.

What always struck Sheldon about Americans was how quickly they assumed intimacy. He knew their curiosity wasn't malicious, but in Europe, small talk felt invasive. A stranger's smile or question about your job could feel like an interrogation.

He pushed his empty plate aside. "What unnerves me is how people act when the law legitimizes bad behavior."

"You mean the Nazis?" Ben asked.

"No, I mean the State."

"That Hitler declared a state of emergency and seized power?"

"Yes, but he was already Chancellor when the Reichstag fire happened. That's not the part that bothers me."

"Then what is?"

Sheldon looked out the window. "Here, it's legal to make a man sit in the back of the bus because of the color of his skin. Most people accept it. McCarthy ruins lives without a shred of evidence. I watched children swear loyalty oaths on the Boston Common, little hands raised. That started with FDR, and Truman kept it going. It wasn't a camp, but it felt the same."

Ben set aside his water. "Saying those kids are the American version of Hitler Youth?"

Sheldon shook his head. "No. Not the same boots. But the same sound."

"What sound?"

"Conformity." He tapped the table. "The quiet kind. The kind that sounds like order, but leads to silence when windows break. Kristallnacht didn't begin with glass—it began with obedience."

They left the diner, walked across the parking lot to the car.

Ben said, "Thought about what you said about breaking glass."

"And?"

"I don't think fascism could take root here."

Sheldon said, "Germans said the same thing: said not in a country that had given the world Bach, Beethoven, and Brahms."

They entered the car, and Ben shifted gears, trying to lighten the mood. "There's something I want to show you."

"What?"

"Bush Terminal. I own a building there."

Sheldon played dumb. He knew the name as a sprawl of waterfront warehouses, once used by the military. Ben described the Gowanus and New York Bay, the proximity to rail and port, how New Jersey sat across the way. But Sheldon saw through it. This wasn't a tour. This was a pitch. Something was in play.

"I have a problem there," Ben said, "and it's bureaucracy. You know why?"

"Why?"

"There's a *papierschnitzel* in Permits and Licenses who's blocking me."

"Go to the next available window."

Ben shook his head. "It's not about a window. It's about him. He runs the department. And he doesn't like my kind."

"You're saying he's an anti-Semite?"

"He's made it clear: Jews should be scrutinized before touching government property."

"Because of the Rosenbergs?"

"Exactly. Julius worked at a military installation in Jersey. Now we all pay the price."

"So what's your plan?"

Ben gave a bitter laugh. "Bribe him? I tried. But now I'm looking at a divorce, and my ship's sinking fast. He's bleeding me dry so one of his friends can steal the land for pennies."

"How?"

"Doesn't matter that I own the building or if it's occupied or not. He's denied the permit, so no business for me, and then there's the property taxes with interest. If I default, the city sells it. The divorce has tagged all my assets, so I can't sell a thing."

"You have something to sell?" Sheldon asked.

"A business in Europe, two machines that could fetch a pretty penny."

"What kind of machines, and why a pretty penny?

"Xerox machines. Couple hundred pounds of dead weight, but that's not what makes them valuable." Ben looked to Sheldon, a twinkle in his eyes. "Only two machines in all of Iran, and the irony is they're like two lead weights, one for each foot, because of the political instability, the divorce, and the lack of a permit while I wait for the tax bill." He sighed.

"And the interest keeps ticking and buries you," Sheldon said.

"That's the pickle, my friend, and it ain't kosher," Ben said. "The *schtickl* doesn't tickle."

They both laughed. Outside, the trees blurred into green as the car rolled on. Sheldon thought about pickles, about vinegar and salt, and about sour truths that never quite rinse clean.

"May I ask what kind of business?" Sheldon asked.

"Ever heard of UNIVAC and ENIAC?"

"The supercomputers?"

"Yeah. Machines. My bet's on transistors. Vacuum tubes are done."

"Go on."

"Those computers run on magnetic tape. Store everything on it. If I can supply that tape, I can feed my family."

"You've got experience in this?"

Ben grinned. "Not in electronics. But information is a family business.

We're printers."

The more Ben spoke, the clearer it became—he was trying to outswim the tide.

They were minutes from Bush Terminal. Ben would show him the waterfront, maybe treat him to a bite in Sunset Park. But Sheldon already felt this trip was an invitation into someone else's survival plan.

Chapter Eighteen

Ben had emphasized he was a building owner, not a tenant.

As they drove, he pointed out buildings and landmarks to Sheldon, painting a picture of Brooklyn's shifting landscape. The Army Base, he said, was the largest storage warehouse in the world, an industrial heart pumping lifeblood from Gowanus to Bay Ridge. The brick row houses, once home to Scandinavians, Poles, and Irish, now housed Jewish and Italian families. Political and cultural tensions aside, both tribes were Democrats.

Ben cited Mayor Impellitteri as an emblem of this shift—an Italian-American who'd replaced the disgraced O'Dwyer. He skipped over the mob ties.

"You see that?" Ben indicated a warehouse as workers moved crates from trucks. "Food, clothes, discount goods—all of it moves through here."

Sheldon asked about the men in uniform.

"Private police," Ben said. "Waterfront needs them."

"Mob connected?"

Ben shrugged. "Who am I to ask?"

Sheldon leaned in. "If bureaucracy squeezes from above, expect a pinch from below."

Ben didn't answer. He slowed the car and pointed to a cluster of buildings.

"Capitalism comes with perks," he said. "Cafeterias for workers. A restaurant for execs. Food trucks for the rest. Bank, telegraph office, even a hospital."

He put the car in park.

"The thorn in my side is a leprechaun named Shay O'Brien."

Sheldon studied him. Ben had pushed his hat back; worry creased his brow.

"You can't get more Irish than that."

Ben said, "I'd let him have his pot o' gold, but I need that permit."

"Has he named a price?"

"Tried and tried, but no."

"Hinted?"

"Nothing."

"Has he threatened violence?"

Ben gripped the wheel. "He's not shanty Irish."

"But people are known to play rough." Sheldon continued, "O'Brien's got power, and you're vulnerable, with the divorce, lawyers, and then there's your daughters. Sure he isn't fishing for a higher price?"

"Nope."

"Then assume the worst. They wait until you're desperate, then offer pennies for your building. You refuse. Maybe it's a trip to Jamaica Bay." Sheldon glanced down at the man's pregnant belly. "And they make sure you don't float."

Ben turned pale. Mission accomplished. Sheldon shifted tone.

"I'm hungry. Know a place?"

Ben offered Peter Luger's. "Six miles, thirty minutes if we're lucky."

Sheldon quipped, "Boston's the same. Two zigzags when you could've walked straight."

* * *

At the steakhouse, Sheldon admired the exposed wood, brass chandeliers, and Germanic charm, which reminded him of Jacob Wirth's in Boston. The place felt more Old World than Brooklyn.

"Worried about kosher?" Ben asked. "Rib cuts only. Even the Orthodox rabbis give it a pass."

They were seated. Ben ordered beer. Sheldon declined. "Enjoy. I'll drive later."

"You don't drink?"

"I have my vices."

Ben grinned. "A man of mystery."

Steaks were ordered, drinks arrived. Sheldon excused himself and made a collect call from a phone booth near the restrooms.

"Jack? It's Sheldon. He's on the hook."

"Where are you?"

"Peter Luger's. You've got three hours to meet him, if you move fast."

Sheldon named a diner upstate and suggested he fly into Newark or find an airfield.

"Stretch the meal out for me."

"Sure thing," Sheldon said. "I'll chew slow, talk more. Maybe order dessert."

"Got a name for his hook?"

"Shay O'Brien. State employee. Controls permits."

"Got it," Jack said. "And the property?"

"Warehouse Bush Terminal in Industrial City."

"Any other color for leverage?"

"Divorce in progress. Worth a judge."

"What else?" Jack asked.

"He might have two Xerox machines for sale. Tehran."

Sheldon could feel the smile over the wires. Jack thanked him, and Sheldon hung up.

* * *

Back at the table, Ben was halfway through his beer.

"You said you were a tailor in a past life. Help me dress better?"

"Try slacks that taper, shirts that fit. Nothing loud."

Ben chuckled. "What else?"

"Confidence. That's what people remember."

Their steaks arrived. As they dug in, Ben hesitated. "Can I ask something sensitive?"

"You want to know more about the camp."

Ben nodded. "I'm sorry. It's a terrible topic over a meal."

"Don't apologize. Curiosity is normal." Sheldon put down his knife. "I was a *sonderkommando*."

He explained that meant ushering the doomed into the gas chambers, removing bodies, cremating the dead. He mentioned that the Nazis purged witnesses like him often to cover their crime.

Ben stared into his beer. "How did you survive?"

"I shut something off inside of me. Some people want to hear philosophy and poetry. I tell them the truth."

Sheldon told a story of the train through empty countryside, birch trees that smelled of smoke. Of babies and old men who never made it inside.

"You ever hear the sound of a mother when she loses her child? It'd make you wonder if God exists."

He described the fabled tale of a prisoner seeing a loved one in the line. He joins them. They die together.

"That story comforts people. But it's a myth."

"No heroics?"

"No choices."

He told how Jews bartered and betrayed. How Nazis killed their own first—testing methods on the disabled before perfecting them on others.

"Savages," Ben said.

"And cruel," Sheldon said. "The writer Remarque fled Germany. Hitler executed his sister out of spite. Then sent the family a bill for her arrest, detention, legal costs, and for what it cost the executioner to sharpen the blade of the guillotine." Sheldon stood. "I should call Tania. Let her know we'll be late."

"Go ahead," Ben said. "And Sheldon—thanks for answering a difficult question."

"Order another beer. We'll talk fashion when I'm back."

Chapter Nineteen

en did enjoy that second beer, and Sheldon bought time for Jack. After checking his watch, Ben suggested they hit the road.

"I said I'd drive," Sheldon said. "Safer for you to ride shotgun."

"Last call to the little boy's room," Ben said, rising unsteadily. Sheldon reached to steady him. "I'm fine."

"Use the men's room. Keys, please."

Ben surrendered them. "I feel embarrassed."

"Why? We had a good lunch, a nice conversation. Guilt is a useless emotion." Sheldon lifted his chin. "Go tinkle. I'll pay the bill."

Ben pulled out his wallet. "Let's go halfsies."

"And spend your ex-wife's money?"

Ben smiled. "She can't be my ex fast enough."

Sheldon refused the money. "I'll meet you outside."

Sheldon lingered at the table while Ben used the restroom. When he paid at the register, Ben passed behind him and walked outside. Sheldon talked to the Italian waiter at the till.

"You could've left it on the table," the young man said.

"I'm new to the area," Sheldon replied. "Didn't want to risk it."

They both knew it was nonsense. Sheldon placed two piles of cash on the counter.

"Why two stacks?"

"One's for the house. The other's your tip. College plans?"

"Brooklyn College." His fingers on the second set of bills. "Thanks, that's generous."

"You work hard. I can tell." Sheldon noticed Ben outside and a trio of punks.

"Yankees or Dodgers?" he asked the kid.

"What do you think?"

Sheldon smiled. "Had to ask." He pointed to the Brooklyn Daily Eagle on the counter. "Mind if I buy that off you?"

"Take it, compliments of the house. Safe travels."

Outside, the sun was blinding, and Ben stood frozen. Three teens orbited him like sharks. Sheldon rolled the newspaper into a club in his hand. The punks hadn't seen him. They poked and taunted Ben, calling him a kike, demanding his wallet. Ben wheeled, disoriented, and tipsy.

Sheldon waited, still as Gary Cooper in *High Noon*. One punk spotted him. "Got somewhere to be, Mister?"

"I'm where I'm supposed to be."

"Then shove off."

"Afraid I can't."

"Why not?"

"That's my friend."

The leader laughed. "This tub of lard? Then you're a Jew, too."

"What's your issue with Jews?"

"You people are moving in, taking over—black hats, beards, the works."

"Notice that my friend and I don't dress that way."

"Yeah, well, he said he's a Jew."

Sheldon nodded. "Orthodox Jews dress that way."

"So you're not Orthodox. Big deal."

"Nothing like ignorance on fire."

"You want to say that up close?"

"Come over here and educate me. You look like public school material."

The punk smirked, then stepped forward. His buddy joined, flicking open a switchblade.

Sheldon's eyes moved between the two of them. A part of him drifted, somewhere far from this moment. He had been here before, only different faces, a different place, a different time. A dark time. A sound echoed in his ears, but it wasn't the boy's knife. It was the sound of a gas chamber door sliding shut.

He exhaled slowly. His body was here, but part of his mind had shut itself off. His hands were steady, controlled. His eyes moved to the blade.

"Your grip's all wrong," Sheldon said. "Wrap your thumb around the handle."

When the kid glanced down, distracted, Sheldon jabbed the rolled up paper into his eye, then swung and hit the other tough in the throat. They crumpled.

He turned to the third. "Your call."

The last kid ran.

* * *

Ben mumbled directions to the highway. Sheldon followed them, switched on the radio. They drove for nearly an hour before Ben spoke.

"What the hell was that?"

"What was what?"

"Back there."

"There were two things at that scene: one, a victim. Two, someone who wasn't."

"There were three of them."

"I refuse to be a victim. Never again."

"This isn't Nazi Germany. This isn't a camp. This is America. We have laws." Ben paused, then added, "Sorry. I shouldn't have lost my temper. Thank you."

"You should get angry more often, Ben. You're right—this isn't Germany. Don't forget, 'law and order' is what made Hitler possible. People obeyed without question."

"Americans are different."

"Are they?" Sheldon asked. "What shows do you watch?"

Ben blinked. "What?"

"Sheldon repeated his question. "TV shows. Which ones?"

"*I Love Lucy. Dragnet.* Why?"

"One says marriage is funny. The other says justice always wins. The fact that they're entertainment should tell you something."

"Relax. They're shows."

"I don't want to relax. Those kids could've hurt you."

Sheldon thought back to the altercation. That switchblade. It had stirred something in him. Adrenaline. The brief rush of controlled rage.

They rode in silence another thirty minutes. Sheldon mentioned needing a bathroom, suggested a quick pie and coffee. Ben agreed.

They pulled into a diner lot. Another car was there—a dark Packard Patrician. Inside, Sheldon spotted Jack Marshall's silhouette.

A bell jingled as they entered the eatery. Cold air wrapped around them. The waitress gestured. "Pick a table."

Sheldon led them to a booth. Ben sat. "Thought you needed the restroom?"

"I do."

"Want to order first?"

"Yes and no."

Ben looked puzzled. The waitress brought menus.

There was the sound of the bell, of someone entering the diner.

"Order me apple pie à la mode," Sheldon said. "Tell her to bring it in five minutes."

"Stomach off?"

"No. Follow the instructions."

Ben shrugged. "What's with you?"

"Do you see the man who came in?"

Ben glanced. Jack nodded.

"I see him."

"When I leave for the restroom, he'll come talk to you."

"About what?"

"Shay O'Brien. A solution. His name is Jack, and he can help you."

"Help how?"

"Legal and money troubles. He'll take care of your problems."

"What is this? Who are you?"

"Not important. Just listen to him. There will be an offer, a trade."

"Trade?" Ben stuttered. "Is this legal?"

Sheldon tapped the table. "Five minutes. Sit and listen to the man."

Chapter Twenty

Leslie led the way to the counter, where they secured tickets for the train to Milan. From there, they would take either a regional line or a taxi to Cadorna Station. MI6 had chosen Asso near Lake Como for the meeting. God's country. The irony of their choice wasn't lost on Walker. To reach it, they'd need a boat to Piona Abbey, perched on the northern tip of the lake.

Leslie had remarked the location was MI6's subtle reminder to 'know their place.' Walker would've called it minding their Ps and Qs.

Clare Boothe Luce had phoned the night before with the details. MI6 had selected the abbey, and the Vatican would provide a car to Lugano afterward. Someone would stand in for Norman Darbyshire, who was in Tehran. Luce added, almost gleefully, that Dulles found MI6's geographic rebuke amusing. The abbey, she said, was built on the Olgiasca, a land formation jutting into the lake like a crooked middle finger.

Walker waited by the wall with their bags while Leslie handled the tickets. The sun was already beating down, promising a humid Roman afternoon. He hoped the train ride might offer some scenic views and maybe a less guarded Leslie. She seemed distracted, either by the mission or the looks she received from the station's local wildlife.

She returned with the tickets.

"*Sei pronto?*"

"No idea what that means," he said, grabbing their bags. He caught sight of a few men laughing.

"They saw me pay," Leslie said. "To them, that's the man's job."

"Well, at least I'm carrying the bags. Do I get points for that?"

"Yeah, Pullman porter points."

"Great. I won't ask for a tip."

She smiled. "Wasn't last night enough fun?"

"It was."

She'd endured another round of catcalls. "Dogs will bark," she said, her voice level.

"Dogs?"

"Men who confuse me with Eve and think they're Adam."

Leslie wasn't dressed provocatively. She wore a yellow dress and sensible shoes. Stylish, yes, but tame. Her sunglasses, resembling Ray-Bans, were custom-made: the arms doubled as tools, as in a screwdriver and a knife. Her steps were deliberate, controlled.

As they walked, a man let out a wolf-whistle loud enough to stop traffic. Leslie didn't even glance his way—until he added something filthy in Italian. Even Walker, who understood almost none of the language, sensed the obscenity. She had sized up her prey like a lioness.

"I'll handle this," she said and stopped.

Her pace slow but sure. The man was polishing an apple, too distracted to notice her approach. She smiled and held out her hand, accepting the fruit without a second thought. She bit into it, savoring the crunch, and then locked eyes with him.

Before he could respond, she shoved the apple into his mouth, pressed him roughly against the wall, and whispered something that made his eyes widen. She released him and walked away, her steps not breaking rhythm.

Walker blinked. "What the hell did you say to him?"

"Something about how apples pair well with pork."

"Subtle."

"Men like him never change."

"You're tense," he observed, following her across the station. "That guy wouldn't normally get to you."

"It's nothing."

"In my experience, when a woman says nothing—"

"Careful, Walker."

He let it drop, but his mind lingered on the edge to her voice. Something wasn't right.

They boarded the train without another word, and soon the familiar motion of the Settebello, a first-class sleeper, relaxed them. The landscape outside was mostly flat farmland, with occasional stretches of vineyards. Walker pulled out his book: *The Old Man and the Sea.* Leslie glanced over and quoted Faulkner: "Hemingway never met a word that might send a reader to a dictionary."

She was reading *Waiting for Godot*, in French.

"La-dee-dah," he'd said.

They settled into the slow, rhythmic hum of the train, gliding through the Italian countryside, and Walker glanced at Leslie again. She was still distant, absorbed in her book. He had his own reservations about what was coming, about the job. It was MI6, after all. Nothing ever went according to plan, not really.

They lunched in the dining car around noon. The train's sleek restaurant car—blue leather, pale yellow walls, sunlight cutting sharp through the windows—felt like a set from a propaganda reel. Walker found it hard to believe anyone traveled this way for leisure.

They split a salad, a veal chop in white wine, and fresh fruit for dessert.

Leslie nibbled a pear, flipping through *Epoca* without reading it. Her glass of wine was nearby. "How are you going to tell them?" she asked, not looking up.

"Tell who what?"

"The change in funding. You think Darbyshire's man is going to take it well?"

Walker shrugged. "He's in the field, right?"

"He is." She glanced up. "And it's Norm, not Norman."

"Ah. Familiar enough with him to call him Norm."

She gave a little shrug. "Ancient history."

Walker raised an eyebrow, amused. "You two?"

"He irons his T-shirts. I found that disturbing."

Walker shook his head. "Norm's proxy will have to accept what we'll tell him."

"He'll push back," she said. "New money means new strings."

"I'll say it's a joint operation," he replied. "Which is a lie. But a polite one."

The stem of her wine glass between two fingers. "There's a word for that."

"Diplomacy?"

"Bureaucracy."

Walker glanced out the window. The lake shimmered in the distance. "You trust him?"

"Norm?" she asked. "I trust that he wants to be the smartest person in the room. Does that help?"

Walker nodded. "Not the same as trust, though."

"No," she agreed. "But it's enough for today."

"Anything else I should expect?"

"The abbey's known for a liqueur called *Gocce Imperiali*. Think Sambuca, but meaner. It'll kill a cold and strip paint off a car."

* * *

Their contact was easy to spot—British to the bone, despite his plain clothes. He didn't approach them. He made them come to him, like a maître d' making the point subtle. The operation. British versus American.

Leslie countered. She chatted with Walker for some time. Eventually, the man approached, took a bag, and said, "This way," in crisp English.

He helped Leslie into a sleek Riva speedboat, leaving Walker to board solo. Walker didn't mind. He admired the mahogany and green paint.

They zipped across Lake Como, slowing only as they neared the abbey. No monks greeted them. That was intentional. No witnesses.

Inside, a man puffed on a Romeo y Julieta cigar.

"There's sherry if you fancy it," he said. "I trust the train was pleasant."

Leslie responded politely.

He turned to Walker. "You're Jack Marshall's man?"

"I am."

"Sit if the spirit moves you."

They sat. The cigar's scent lingered—sweet and woody.

"Let's cut to the chase," the Brit said. "What's the message from the old man in Rome?"

"You want it straight?" Walker asked.

"Please. Subtlety isn't your strong suit."

"Amazing you can smoke with your head that far up your own ass."

The man's eyes bulged. "Pardon?"

"I meant arse—so you'd understand."

He turned to Leslie. "You jumped ship for this?"

"No, lack of career advancement. A woman likes to feel appreciated."

"Fair enough," their host said, then back to Walker. "So what's changed?"

"Funding."

"Her Majesty's money no good?"

"Her February message to the Shah caused confusion."

"How so?"

"It was sent from the RMS Queen Elizabeth. He didn't know if it was from the monarch or the ocean liner. Took Prime Minister Eden to clean it up."

"And Dulles exploited it," the man said.

"Yes."

"Darbyshire's the best man on the ground."

"No argument there."

"Then what's the issue?"

"There isn't one."

Pause. Smoke. "So money talks."

"Didn't it always?"

The Brit exhaled. "Typical of you Americans."

"I'm not here for thanks or favors. There's a job to be done."

"Who delivers the money?"

"Roosevelt."

"Kim?" The Brit stood. "He's as brash as a Hollywood mogul. Precision matters."

Walker rose, too. "Precision? Like Dresden? Firebombing a city into ash counts as precision now?" He kept his voice level. "I've seen Milan, too. British precision is carved into the walls there, too. None of it was as glamorous as Hollywood, but it sparked a hell of a resistance, so, cheers and thank you. Roosevelt is the man."

"We're done here."

"Oh, one last thing," Walker said.

The man huffed. "What is it?"

"Tell Churchill he should stick to painting. Maybe capture the decline of the empire."

The Brit gave a tight smile. "I'll pass it along."

As he left, his cigar smoke curled behind him like a final insult.

Chapter Twenty-One

Leslie and Walker stepped out into the alpine light, the breeze off the lake clean and cold. Below, the water shimmered like silver foil. Still, but never quiet.

A cardinal in a dark coat handed Leslie the keys to a Lancia Spider. She spoke briefly in Italian with the man, crisp and low, then turned back. Walker barely had time to react before Leslie was already in motion.

"Coming?" she said.

She stood at the driver's side, expectant. "Can you handle a right-hand drive?"

"No."

"Thought so."

She slid behind the wheel like she'd done it a hundred times.

* * *

The road to Lugano wound through hills and terraced villas. They'd been driving ten minutes when Walker noticed the Fiat. "Behind us."

Leslie didn't look. "I saw."

A silver Fiat 1100 kept its distance but didn't bother hiding.

"Do you know who he is?"

"MI6." Leslie checked the mirror. "His car's no match for us, though."

The Lancia was red as dried blood. Sleek, fast, and quiet. It could outrun the Fiat twice over. Walker looked back. The man behind the wheel was tall, blond, sunglasses, set jaw.

"Did His Eminence say something to you when he handed you the keys?" Walker asked and waited. Leslie offered a brief phrase in Italian. Walker waited for the translation.

"He told me when to open the engine." She dropped a gear.

The car rocketed forward. A sharp curve, a spin to face their tail, and then a full stop. Dust kicked up behind the Lancia and in front of the Fiat.

The Fiat braked hard. Leslie reached into her purse for a .380 and eased the door open.

"Let's get this over with," she said.

The man stepped out. Something about him said ex-military, likely SAS. He raised his hands, palms exposed, and did a slow clockwise rotation to show that he was unarmed.

Leslie kept the pistol angled low. "State the message."

"Not so much a message, more like frustration."

"Yours?"

"And others."

"Is that supposed to mean something?"

"Old friends are watching. You're not the only ones at the table."

Leslie gestured toward Walker. "He's the lead."

"Is he?"

He gave Walker a long, hard look. "Walker, right?"

"That's right."

"You up for this?"

"That an official inquiry, or just friendly concern?"

"No. I have a long memory. I've seen what happens when the wrong man is at the wheel, and from the looks of it, you're not driving. She is."

"You don't say. Anything else?"

"People die for the wrong reasons."

Leslie said nothing.

One last thing." He took a breath. "No matter how clean the plan, there's always sand in your shoes." He waited. "Sand sticks. Biblical."

He turned, got into the Fiat, and was gone.

* * *

Lugano came into view, the lake a deep blue sapphire cut into the mountains. More Amalfi than Bern. Sunlight, villas, and the kind of silence only money could afford.

No cuckoo clocks. No postcards.

They didn't speak. What lay ahead—and what they'd left behind—settled between them like weather.

Rumors clung to the hills. Nazis in hiding. Gold in vaults. Silence for sale. Amnesia that paid interest.

They had a name. A villa. A meeting.

Reinhard Gehlen was Hitler's man in the East. Shrewd, cold, unreadable. Jack Marshall once called him a cross between a chameleon and a crocodile.

He'd crawled out of the rubble offering treasure: names, maps, Soviet technology. No one knew what were jewels and what was paste—but no one dared call his bluff.

From Bormann's old estate in Bavaria, he built The Org. Staffed it with SS leftovers and other survivors of every purge. Men with steady hands and empty eyes.

Gehlen didn't adapt to the new world. He built it.

Leslie pulled the Lancia into a quiet turnout overlooking the lake. Ahead, the funicular climbed the hillside like a private toy for a rich man. Silent, slow, inevitable.

Walker watched it. He thought of Angels Flight in LA, then let it go.

"Typical MI6," Leslie said. "Show you the mountain. Hand you the rope."

At the villa's lower gate, Walker scanned. "No security."

"Look again."

He did. Small movements behind hedges. Shadows at the roofline. Nothing overt. Everything covered.

"Think they'll play rough?" he asked.

"This is theater. Sit still. Watch the show. Don't flinch."

He nodded, quietly. Then, almost absently: "Had a date once. Her father made me come in through the mudroom. There were dogs."

CHAPTER TWENTY-ONE

Leslie gave a half-smile. "What happened?"

"He stared the whole meal. Never said a word."

"And the girl?"

"Didn't last."

She looked at the villa, the stone walls soaking in the sun. "Same story here."

Then, glancing at him, "Only this time, we bring the wine."

Chapter Twenty-Two

She was 'G' for Guest—meaning Gentile. It was the truth, minus the color, and what stung was that Judith had fallen victim to peer pressure. She had ignored Tania, and the frost was unexpected and inexplicable. Tania was not unaccustomed to fickle teenagers. She'd adapt to the coldness from Judith.

Tania ate breakfast alone. She tried. She'd say hello to others. Received a few mumbled replies, a plastic smile or two. She ignored it until she berated herself for caring.

She slipped back into old skin, did what the hunted and ostracized do. She observed.

The queen bees arrived.

Tania gauged them immediately. This girl gang wore the same muted blue uniform, moved in formation. Esther Pomerantz led the pack, a wannabe Elizabeth Taylor with her haughty gaze and choreographed hips. Her second was a pint-sized Audrey Hepburn impersonator, lips coral-pink before and after breakfast. The third was busty and bleached, who provided the comic relief, a Marilyn type who'd never risk a swim. Too much chlorine, not enough attention.

Someone loomed at Tania's elbow. Miriam Moskowitz.

"That's Esther Pomerantz and her Pomeranians."

"Pomeranians?"

"Not to their faces, of course. Pomeranians is a play on Esther's last name. They think pom-poms are cute."

"You don't?"

Miriam peeled a speck of shell from a boiled egg.

"The word for them I'd use is appropriate to a kennel."

Tania smirked. "Who made them royalty?"

"No one had to die. They just declared it."

"I bet the boys love them."

"Lust is more accurate."

Tania tuned out the list of names and fathers' occupations. She was more interested in their behavior than their pedigree. This was a pack. And Esther was alpha.

"What do the boys say about Esther?"

"Depends who you ask."

"How about the girls in her circle?"

"Everything from 'Daddy's paying for a nose job' to 'She does everything but…'"

Tania was ready to rise from her seat.

One of the Pomeranians had slipped something into Judith's drink.

She crossed the dining hall.

Esther turned. "I don't believe we've met."

"Tania. I need to speak with Judith."

Esther tilted her head theatrically. "How very direct."

"It's important."

Esther gave the nod, and her entourage eased away, in a slow procession, every girl casting a sideways sneer as they passed Tania.

Judith remained. "I can't imagine what's so urgent."

"Don't drink your orange juice."

"Why not?"

"One of them put something in it."

Judith looked from Tania to the glass.

"Don't drink it, Judith."

Judith downed the glass in a single gulp. She handed it to Tania. "Here. Since you're so concerned."

Tania held the glass up to the light. No fizz, no color change.

She sniffed. Nothing. That didn't mean harmless. Some things took time to work.

* * *

Later, back in her room, she searched for a book. Thomas Mann had stayed behind in Boston. Sheldon's orders were 'No German.' She picked up *The Price of Salt* by Claire Morgan and *The Sea Wall* by Marguerite Duras. She chose Duras for the setting of French Indochina, and because she'd overheard Sheldon and Jack Marshall arguing about Truman and Eisenhower feeding funds to the French. 'A future unwinnable war,' Sheldon said. 'A hotspot,' Jack declared.

Tania wandered back into the social fray, where women and girls were locked in generational combat over music. Grandmothers taught the Charleston; daughters demanded the Jive. The youngest raved about a new song, *Crazy Man, Crazy* by Bill Haley and His Comets.

Tania tuned them out. Duras' tale of poverty and despair was more gripping.

A boy tried to lure her to a pool exercise class.

"No thanks," she said.

"I might have to give you puppy eyes."

"Nice try. What you really want is to see me in a swimsuit."

"I bet you look swell."

"If you like a white nose full of zinc."

"Wouldn't matter to me."

"Well, here's a tip, Romeo."

"What's that?"

"Make sure your next victim has a pulse."

"Ouch. You cut a guy deep."

He left with a wink, calling her Juliet as he went.

She returned to her book. Duras reminded her of Thomas Mann's *Die Betrogene*—*The Deceived*—mistranslated as *The Black Swan*. Both stories about delusion. But Duras added hunger, heat, and humiliation.

A shadow fell across the page.

CHAPTER TWENTY-TWO

It was Ruth.

Tania sat up, ready to smile until she saw the fear on the girl's face. "What is it?"

"It's Judith. She's sick."

"She's in the bathroom," Ruth said, voice breaking. "She's afraid to move."

Tania stood. "Take me to her."

"She's humiliated because you were right."

"She shouldn't be."

"She is," Ruth choked. "It's worse."

Tania paused. "What do you mean?"

Ruth swallowed hard. "The Pom-Poms."

Tania nodded. "They spiked her drink."

Ruth shook her head. "It's worse than that." She looked away, voice cracking. "They took all the toilet paper. From every stall."

Tania stood still. Her stomach dropped. This wasn't about humiliating Judith. It was about trapping her.

"She's in there alone," Ruth whispered. "And sick."

Chapter Twenty-Three

Tania moved fast; her shoes clicked sharply on the floor. She fished a five-dollar bill from her clutch, her fingers moist from the summer's night air, and approached a housekeeper in the hallway.

"A roll of toilet paper, and in a discreet bag, please."

The woman hesitated, her brow furrowed, but Tania's eyes were steady, unblinking. She opened her mouth to refuse the money, but Tania slid the bill into her shoulder strap with a practiced ease.

"Take it," Tania said, her tone soft but insistent. "In case someone accuses you of theft."

The woman nodded, accepting the bribe with a stiff smile.

Ruth led the way. Tania followed, but her mind was already ahead, calculating the next move. They reached the bathroom. Tania locked the door behind them and leaned against the wall, eyes on the stall. She heard Judith's groans. "It's me, Judy."

"Tania?" Her voice barely a whisper. "I don't know what to do. This is awful."

Tania detected the faint stench of sweat, nausea, and what was expected in the humid air. The odor, sharp and uncomfortable, like unchanged hospital linens.

"I'll be right back. Give her this." Tania handed Ruth the roll of paper and a small perfume atomizer, its floral scent a stark contrast to the room's oppressive air. "Tell her it's from London. She'll like it."

Ruth nodded, confused but obedient. Tania nudged her, while her mind raced ahead.

The hallway buzzed with idle voices and the music, polite. Tania moved, but slower now, her pace measured. Ahead was the bar. Behind her, a girl in a stall, sick and humiliated. She stopped. She thought for a second. Judy was not her problem.

She caught her reflection in a wall sconce's mirrored backplate. Lipstick fine. Hair in place. Eyes clear. Decide now, follow through or not. Maybe it mattered. Maybe doing one decent thing, without an angle, counted for something.

This wasn't strategy. She wasn't gaining leverage. And still, her feet had turned toward the bar, already calculating the things needed to provide comfort. She exhaled. Just once.

Then she kept moving.

Tania moved through the crowd near the bar, the low hum of conversation in the air. The bartender spared her a glance, but she had caught his attention. Though beauty was an armor and intimidated men, she knew helplessness and urgency appealed to the chivalric.

"Tonic with a splash of bitters," she ordered.

"That all, miss?"

She slid a few bills toward him. "Have any peppermint or ginger candy?"

"Starlight mints from my stash. That okay?"

"Perfect."

He handed her a small paper bag. As he did, a middle-aged man sidled up, too close for comfort, his breath warm and stale with Pepsodent and cheap cologne.

"You know the drinking age is eighteen in New York?" he said, leaning in slightly.

"I wasn't ordering alcohol."

He leaned in further, his scent heavy in her nostrils. "So, you're one of those modern, progressive girls I've been reading about."

"You read?"

He straightened up, surprised, but she wasn't done. She didn't let him close the gap.

He shrugged. "I do, indeed."

The bartender returned with her order, but the man didn't leave. He lingered, watching her like a predator sizing up his prey.

"Strange drink."

"Old remedy for an upset stomach for a friend of mine."

"Kind of you. Allow me to buy you a real drink."

Tania barely looked at him. "Do you have daughters?"

"I do. Why?"

She raised an eyebrow, her gaze never faltering. "Older or younger than me?"

"You haven't said how old you are."

"Pretend I'm eighteen. Now answer the question."

"One younger, one older. Your point?"

Tania took a slow sip from the complimentary glass of water the barkeep had set on the counter, keeping her eyes on him. "How would you feel if a man like you came sniffing around them?"

The man blinked, clearly thrown off guard.

"I didn't proposition you."

"But you thought it." A faint curve to her lips, she smiled. "Your girls might be underage or legal, but I was doing illegal things at both ages."

"You're a spitfire then."

"I'm worse. This doll is broken and dangerous."

With that, she turned away and returned to the bathroom, knowing the man wouldn't follow. He would retreat to his corner, nurse his bruised ego.

She knocked twice, the sound sharp and deliberate. Ruth opened the door.

"She's still in there," Ruth said, her voice tight with fear. "She's unwell."

Tania slipped inside, carrying the drink and the bag of mints.

Judith emerged from the stall, pale, hair messy and damp. She was the epitome of discomfort, her body language stiff but weak.

Tania stepped closer, her hand outstretched with the tonic. "If I'd known, I'd have brought ice," she said softly.

Judith didn't respond, but accepted the drink, hands shaky. She gulped it down quickly, like it might soothe a scorched throat.

"Peppermint helps nausea," Tania said, her voice steady. "I've got mints, too."

Judith nodded weakly, her face strained. "Ruth, give us a minute?"

The door clicked shut behind Ruth, leaving the two of them in the cramped room. Judith stared at her, searching for something—answers, maybe. Or a reason to trust her.

"I don't know what kind of game you're playing," Judith said, voice low.

Tania let the words hang in the air. No rush.

"There's no game," she said. "You have to believe me."

"Something's off about you, like you're up to something. You and your uncle seem awfully interested in my father."

"If you haven't noticed, Judy, this place isn't hospitable to strangers."

"I can't lay my finger on it."

Judith's gaze was piercing, but Tania held it. "I heard you and Sheldon whispering."

Tania slowly unwrapped a mint, offering it to Judith. "It's a secret," she said, her words low but careful. "Just not the kind you think."

"Try me."

Tania hesitated, then leaned in slightly. "The government wants something your father owns or controls. I don't know all the details. Sheldon's the go-between."

"Why not just ask him?"

"They can't. Not directly."

Judith's brow furrowed. "That sounds shady."

"It might be," Tania said, her voice steady. "But what they want is legitimate. The reason they want it? I haven't a clue. Honest."

Judith shook her head. "Governments don't do shady things. People do."

Tania smiled. Judith dabbed her face with a towel. "Thanks for the perfume. I should've listened to you when you warned me not to drink the juice. Esther and those bitches. I think it was laxatives."

Tania nodded. "Laxatives as a Mickey Finn? Brutal."

"And effective." Judith sighed, "Felt like I was standing in water when lightning struck."

"What do they have against you?"

"Nothing," Judith said, her voice small. "They pick a target every summer. My number came up. Lucky me. Once they put Nair into someone's shampoo."

Tania leaned on the sink, listening intently. "And no one stops them?"

"Esther's dad is a bigwig, which is why she gets away with it."

Tania shook her head. "I hear they've never won the talent show."

Judith snorted. "That's their holy grail. It's Esther's dream to do a solo act that wins the trophy and cash prize."

Tania raised an eyebrow. "You ever enter?"

"God, no. Ruth has talent. I don't. I tried once. A Jolson number."

"What song?"

"*When the Red, Red Robin*. It was tragic."

"I bet you were adorable."

"I wasn't. Never again."

Tania ran the cold water and told Judy to keep her wrist under the stream. She said it'd give her nerves some relief from the heat.

Their eyes met, the air between them thick with something unspoken. "Want revenge?"

Judith smiled.

And didn't say no.

Chapter Twenty-Four

The storm hadn't left. And neither had Tania. She sat in the chair by Judith's bed, eyes half-closed but mind awake. Always awake. Ruth had slept nearby and disappeared by the time Judith woke up.

"Ever had Jewish cabin fever?" Judith asked.

"Is that a real thing?" Tania said.

"Welcome to the Catskills—home of Rip Van Winkle and the Headless Horseman."

She flung off the covers. Her father and Ruth were still asleep, and she wanted first crack at the shower. Contrary to the complaint men had about women, Judith said her father was the one who took forever in the bathroom.

She threw on a light gown and gave Tania three choices: join her, wait her turn, or head back to her own room. Judith didn't seem worried about Tania being caught in her room.

Tania chose to return to her room before Sheldon noticed she was gone, but promised to meet Judith and walk her to breakfast.

As Judith dressed, she talked.

"Funny how kids pray for snow days in the winter. Doesn't work in the summer."

Tania didn't respond. She liked the school year. She earned money tutoring or translating. French was in demand among grad students; Spanish was growing among high schoolers. German was declining, thanks to Hitler and anti-German sentiment from both world wars.

Russian was rare, but when a student trusted her with smuggled samizdat, she felt a thrill. Sometimes it came on carbon paper, other times tissue-thin sheets. To her, they were modern-day archaeological finds. She warned those students to keep their circle small. They joked about the KGB; she reminded them about the CIA, FBI, and the freshly minted NSA.

With Mozart echoing in her head, Tania walked into the breakfast hall alone. Rain sheeted the windows. Distant lightning cracked the sky, followed by thunder that reminded her of Strauss's *Also sprach Zarathustra*.

She spotted Sheldon deep in conversation with his new friend Ben.

Moments later, Judith and Ruth arrived. Ruth, all enthusiasm and fragments of ideas, rattled off possible talent show acts. Judith reminded her the lottery hadn't been drawn yet.

Several tables sat empty. Some guests, discouraged by the weather, stayed in bed or waited for lunch. Others made good on their prepaid breakfast, piling plates high and brimming with glassware.

Miriam Moskowitz nibbled shirred eggs while her husband, Walter, doctored tomato juice with Worcestershire sauce. Tania recalled how strange English pronunciation was. She didn't know how to say Worcestershire until a Bostonian said 'Worcester.'

Judith barely touched her food, a remnant of last night's cruelty.

Judith introduced Tania to new faces. The group nodded and resumed their chatter. Two men argued over who was tougher in football: Hardy 'The Hatchet' Brown or Chuck Bednarik.

"The Hatchet could tackle a whole backfield and spit out the one with the ball."

"Concrete Charlie could make gangsters cry," his friend countered.

Tania didn't care for sports.

She remembered Sheldon's advice, to listen and observe. Spies and writers used the same tools, only the toolkit changed. She let the noise wash over her.

But she wasn't just listening anymore—she was choosing a side. That was new.

Next, she heard politics.

"I'm telling you—the Marshall Plan was the right move," one man said. "Compassionate. Strategic."

"Nuts. Rebuild Germany? After Hitler?"

"Versailles made Hitler."

"And the same people who gave us Wagner gave us the SS."

"They elected Hitler. Democratically. You want us to turn the other cheek?"

"I didn't say forget."

"Well, maybe we should lie awake thinking about Hiroshima."

"Maybe we should. The Russians have bombs now. The whole world's *meshuggah*."

They agreed on one thing—Truman was right to desegregate the military.

"Jim Crow has to go."

They were less united on McCarthy. One man's wife cited *The Crucible* as a warning.

"And what about Israel?" one asked. "Truman at least recognized it."

"Eisenhower did too."

"Yeah, but will he protect it?"

"What, are we the world's cops now?"

"Hitler made people think we were fleas. Even Jack the Ripper was an anti-Semite."

"Jack the Ripper?"

"He wrote near a victim: 'The Juwes are the men that will not be blamed for nothing.'"

Tania had heard all the tropes, about Jews and money, Irish and drink, Italians and garlic. Here, even grief spoke in Yiddish. She listened to another exchange.

"You read *Forverts*?"

"Of course. Lod, Hadera. Then Kfar Hess. A couple gunned down in their home."

"That's how it starts," he warned.

"How what starts?"

"Until none of us are left."

The lack of sunlight cast the room in grayscale, like an old newsreel. The guests left. Judith and Ruth wandered off, and Sheldon joined Tania.

"Enjoying yourself?"

"How was your road trip?"

"Productive. It's all in Jack's hands now."

"I hope this ends soon and well," Tania said.

"Anxious to leave? I thought you were making friends."

She didn't answer. The Pomeranian pack strutted in. Esther led, her two lackeys close behind. They moved like the room belonged to them. Esther's hips swayed with practiced exaggeration.

Sheldon noticed. "Which one gets under your skin?"

"Esther."

"Read the magazine," he said, tapping her hand. "But don't subscribe."

"What's that supposed to mean?"

"It's their world. You don't live there."

"I'll be gone soon."

"You shouldn't compare yourself to her."

"Who says I do?"

"Then why are you upset?" He looked at Esther. "They're amateurs. They couldn't handle a tenth of what you survived in Vienna. Or is it something else?"

Tania's eyes narrowed. "Something else?"

"Jealousy, maybe?"

"Of her? You can't be serious."

He watched the clique a moment longer. "Ignore them. We'll be out soon enough."

She looked toward Judith and Ruth. "Not soon enough," she said. But her voice had softened.

Across the room, Esther laughed too loudly.

Tania didn't smile.

She'd help Judith win. And make Esther regret ever picking a target.

Chapter Twenty-Five

On the third ring, Leslie answered the phone like Lady Godiva—naked, unapologetic, and bathed in Mediterranean light. Walker propped himself against the pillows, watching her. She listened, nodding silently, responding with soft hums. Then she hung up without a word.

Walker had moved the phone away from the window on purpose earlier. The reasons were layered: to keep her out of sight from the American Embassy across the way, to prevent a photograph from the street below, and, most of all, to deny a sniper a clear shot. No shadows to track, no depth to gauge. Still, he watched her silhouette, tension crawling across his chest like a hangover that hadn't fully landed.

She turned to face him. He took in the view.

Not for the first time, he wished she were less beautiful when she lied.

"Who was that?" he asked.

"A message. For you."

"But this is your room."

"And you, sir, are in it. We're adults, Walker. No need to act like a prude. Your virtue isn't under surveillance. Mother isn't watching."

"My mother's dead."

"You know what I mean."

"Message from whom?"

She looked around the room, including the ceiling. "This place is probably wired."

"Dulles or MI6?"

"Take your pick. Probably both."

"What did the message say?"

"Kermit delivered."

"Was that Norman?"

"No. Our nameless blond friend from the road. He sounded peeved playing messenger."

Walker tossed off the covers, annoyed. "Typical British."

He regretted it the second it left his mouth—sounded too petulant, too American.

Leslie cinched her robe. "Ignore him."

"Because I'm the ugly American?"

"No, because MI6 was running this op before you arrived. Now they've been told to step back. And someone else is footing the bill."

Walker looked at her. "You're defending them?"

His voice was quiet, but the edge was sharp enough to draw blood.

"I'm providing context. Don't be childish."

"And you're not biased, with Norm in the picture."

"I always knew MI6 was involved."

"Then it's Norm."

"I didn't sleep with him, Walker."

"I didn't say that."

"You implied it. Look, this operation predates you."

"You mean me personally, or Americans in general?"

"You. And most Americans can't find Iran on a map."

"Maybe I'm different because we're in Italy. Maybe it's you and old friends."

The accusation was half a joke, but it sat like a stone between them.

She poured water and handed him a glass. "What's with the mood? Regret?"

"For last night?"

"Or the last few nights. Guilt can add up."

"I'm not looking for a fight."

"Good. It's my room. You're in my bed."

He tied his robe. "Anything else in the message?"

She checked her watch. "You're meeting Dulles at ten."

She said it too casually—like it hadn't been waiting in her mouth the whole time.

As if on cue, something slid under the door—an envelope. Sunlight hit it.

Walker retrieved it. "Typed. Who types this early? And you're grinning like the Cheshire Cat."

"Probably no fingerprints. You'd need a lab to tie it to a typewriter. Remind you of Vienna?"

He opened it. "Downstairs. Ten o'clock, like the lady said."

"I'm a lady, now?"

He looked up, with the faintest of smiles at the corner of his mouth. "Depends who's listening."

* * *

Dulles waited at a private table in the back of the Hotel Excelsior's café. A lone waiter served the room. A silent bodyguard sat nearby, still as a statue.

Dulles didn't look up. He was reading the *Alto Adige*, a German-language paper from South Tyrol. In his other hand, a cup of black coffee. His breakfast was gone, save a few crumbs.

Walker slowed his approach—not to be dramatic, but because something about Dulles always made him feel like a student, late to class. Sensing him, Dulles folded the paper and rose. They shook hands.

"I got your message," Walker said.

"Kermit arrived," Dulles confirmed. "I have an update."

"Jack delivered?"

"Through his friend. Everything's in place."

Walker sat. "Do I need to know anything specific?"

"Not yet. You know how this works—it's mostly waiting."

Walker hated waiting.

"Will I be able to contact our British friend?"

"There's a number on your desk upstairs. Tehran's two and a half hours ahead. Once you make contact, set your own schedule. Vary the times."

"No predictable pattern," Walker said. "Got it."

"All calls should be from the Excelsior."

"This hotel?"

"I've used it since '48. Everything's set up."

"While Jack and I were in Vienna, you were here?"

Dulles smiled, faintly. That smile had decades in it, of covert elections, envelopes of cash, forged documents. Walker couldn't decide if it impressed him or made his skin crawl. Behind the expression was a classified chapter in U.S. history. He had helped steer Italy's election, flooding money to the Christian Democrats to push out the Communists.

Catholicism, Conservatism, Capitalism—his three Cs had beaten Communism.

"Is there anything I can do to help Jack?"

"No. You stay put. Run things from the room."

A waiter appeared. Walker ordered a cappuccino and a cornetto. When the waiter left, he asked, "A question?"

Dulles looked up from his coffee and waited.

"Should Leslie be in the room when I speak with Norman?"

"It's your show, Walker. Set the tempo."

Walker hesitated. "Will Kermit follow orders?"

"Why wouldn't he?"

Walker considered lying. He settled for silence.

"What about coordination between Jack's friend and what's happening on the ground?"

"I'll handle that," Dulles said. "From here and from New York."

"New York?" Walker tried to mask surprise. "Where we met?"

Dulles nodded. "One of my people is waiting there. It won't interfere with your show."

"I was thinking rhythm. Coordination."

"It's being handled."

"Anyone I know?"

"You haven't met him, but you know his work. PR man."

"An ad guy?"

"With a translator. He'll write the message; the translator renders it into

CHAPTER TWENTY-FIVE

Farsi."

"Norman speaks Farsi."

"Remind him—we control the message. Not him, not MI6. I'm sure you'll find a diplomatic way to dispatch that memo."

Walker nodded. "These posters and pamphlets can't feel foreign. The translator must sound like a native."

Dulles studied him. For the first time, Walker felt like he was being *read* rather than managed. The pause that followed was surgical.

"Jack said you're a writer."

"And?"

"Writers understand persuasion."

Walker smiled. "We're professional liars then?"

"Govern what's in your sphere. Set the expectation with MI6."

"And the rest?"

"Trust that they'll do their part, Walker."

"Trust?"

"Jack's contact gave us tools in Tehran. It'll handle production. I'll arrange for translations. Kermit provides the money and will handle distribution. Norman controls local resources."

Walker sipped his coffee, holding off on the cornetto. "What if they need more funds?"

"Norman will ask if more coal is needed from Newcastle."

"Coal?"

"Kohle. German slang for money."

Dulles stood, folded his paper, and left.

Walker took a bite of the pastry, its sweetness cutting through the bitter coffee. He felt not relief, not even clarity, but the cold click of inevitability.

The water in the glass shimmered. Not a Rubicon. Not yet.

It was Sarajevo. One spark. One fuse. Continents burned.

He took the glass, drank, and let it begin.

Chapter Twenty-Six

Leslie said she'd join him later downstairs, where they'd meet Dulles and Luce for drinks in the lobby.

He sat at a small table by the window, the glass of Campari and soda in a shallow ring of condensation. The ice melted slowly, the redness of the Italian bitter fading, a ritual with ice.

Outside his window, he viewed a Rome that eased into evening—sultry, smooth, seductive. The Via Veneto shimmered. Summer heat seemed to lift off the cobblestones at dusk. He watched the cars and people: a Lancia Aurelia, then two Vespas, each with a couple on them. The man smiled, his teeth exposed, sunglasses masking his eyes. A delivery boy weaved through traffic on the sidewalk with a crate of peaches. A woman in a navy dress with large buttons passed by, cigarette lit, her exhale unhurried. A man swept a step. A priest savored some gelato.

He turned his attention to the crowd inside. He caught his reflection in a hotel mirror and ran a hand down the front of his shirt. Once, he'd taken pride in his uniform, with three combat decorations for heroism, the paratrooper's patch, most of all the Combat Infantryman's Badge. He'd never imagined a boy from the cornfields of Middle America sitting in a glamorous hotel in Rome, in a white dinner jacket, black trousers, cummerbund, and bow tie. He thought only Cary Grant could pull off the look.

He thought of the actor because across the room, he spotted Gregory Peck and Audrey Hepburn, there to celebrate the wrap of a film. Walker had heard the concierge mention the title *Roman Holiday*.

His reflection reminded him of the distance traveled, the bitterness endured. Lifetimes.

Middle America would've called this Rome decadent, even dangerous. From the pulpit: warnings of foreigners and temptations. A gray world, ambiguous, no clear lines, no right angles.

But Walker had stopped believing in blue skies and that the world stood still.

He had killed. He had seen Dachau. He understood Conrad's *Heart of Darkness*. He was there to have drinks with the Ivy-educated Dulles, the cobra who could charm the charmer.

Still, some part of America had prepared him for this. He came from a town that taught a boy how to hold a gun before a passport. It prepared him for men like Allen W. Dulles—and it didn't. Childhood truths came laminated, printed in church bulletins and campaign flyers. The men at the lunch counter who hadn't left their zip code in forty years could never envision a Dulles. He came from good people—generous, so long as you didn't ask too many questions or forget the flag on the Fourth of July.

He forgot all about Little League when bullets whizzed past his ears.

Rome tilted toward twilight, inevitable as sunrise and sunset. A man tuned a violin beneath a streetlamp. The ancient city carried on as if it couldn't sleep because of the heat.

Dulles and Luce had entered the room, but they didn't see him. Luce, the ambassador, spotted someone she must greet and said as much into Allen's ear. He understood. He always understood. Walker watched. Dulles worked the room with ease, grace, and quiet confidence. He was warm to everyone, attentive, yet attentive to opportunity and weakness. He was a predator in still waters.

Dulles approached a man just shy of his height. At six-two to the other's five-eleven, he'd have the reach if it were boxing, and if professors boxed.

The Italian wasn't what people expected. Not the Mediterranean lover, no Valentino. His ears stuck out slightly, and he carried the stillness of a man more comfortable in libraries than salons. The air of a scholar bent over a book or a map.

Walker stood, left his drink behind. He didn't want to shake hands with a wet mitt. He waded through the crowd, aware Dulles would sense him moving in from behind. He came up on the two men in dinner jackets. Dulles was known for witty conversation, but Walker wondered how humor landed with someone whose first language wasn't English. He knew he'd stumbled in German, which is why he left the Berlitz work to Leslie.

Walker heard the conversation *in medias res*.

"Ah, Signor Ministro Andreotti. They said you were here somewhere. I was worried I wouldn't find you in this storm of people."

"Storms move. I stay put."

A waiter offered champagne. They accepted flutes.

Dulles, eyes unreadable. "I've heard the most reliable reports come from behind the curtain—velvet or otherwise."

Andreotti, without looking up. "Confession is a form of surrender. And usually too late."

"Surrender or not, it's a truth, isn't it?"

Andreotti smiled faintly. "In theory. Like democracy."

Andreotti looked down at the bubbles in his champagne. Nothing escaped this man.

Dulles didn't have time for a rebuttal. The Italian stepped forward and disappeared.

Dulles turned sideways and saw Walker. They shook hands. Dulles whispered that the man was Giulio Andreotti. "He's a necessary weapon to defeat Communism in Italy."

And there it was: Andreotti was one of many tools in the shed.

"Is he our man?" Walker asked.

"If Machiavelli was a Catholic."

Walker didn't have time to unwrap it. Dulles took him by the elbow and guided him to where Hepburn and Peck stood in a field of well-wishers. He had timed it well, as he was last in line to greet them.

Walker idled back, exchanging looks with Audrey while Dulles and Peck spoke. The two men had met before, somewhere. Dulles apologized for the breach in etiquette by greeting Peck first. He kissed her hand and introduced Walker.

Walker stepped forward, then shook hands with Peck after the introduction. Dulles presented Walker to Hepburn.

Peck said, "We leave the world in your hands, Allen, while we pretend it's the Dirty Thirties."

Dulles smiled. "As long as it's not 1939."

"Nice meeting you, Walker."

Audrey kissed Walker on the cheek and whispered: *"Fais attention à toi, mon ami."*

The kiss surprised him. He wished he knew what she had said.

Peck and Hepburn drifted toward the door. Andreotti watched them go, a faint, unreadable smile on his face. Dulles nudged Walker as Leslie entered the lobby.

She wore a Dior New Look dress, all cinched waist and soft shimmer. It struck Walker as wrong. If clothes made the man, then this dress didn't match the woman. Demure, the fabric caught the light so. Leslie was more Carole Lombard: casual, flirtatious, quick with her wit, a storm over water when provoked. The dress whispered femininity; Leslie seldom whispered.

She carried a minaudière with a beaded clasp and moved to the far side of the room with the confidence of someone observing a chessboard, not joining the game. Walker trailed behind, a tugboat out of sync with a luxury liner.

A waiter offered her champagne; she declined, politely.

"You look nice," he said.

"No, I don't. But that's the point."

He was about to ask what she meant when Audrey Hepburn reappeared. She moved through the crowd with purpose and found Clare Boothe Luce near a marble column. The two women greeted one another. Their embrace was part affection, part performance.

Walker and Leslie watched from a distance.

"Look at them," Leslie said. "They're a study in contrast."

Hepburn wore a pale blue Sorelle Fontana, ballet flats, her hair pinned in a ballerina twist. Luce stood grounded in a gray Mainbocher gown. No sparkle. The gamine met the patrician dove.

"Audrey's thanking Clare," Leslie added, eyes never leaving them.

"For what?"

"The dress. The designers are three sisters, local. Audrey's putting them on the map."

Walker considered this. "I thought Luce would be the one doing that."

"Here in Italy, sure. But Audrey?" She opened her minaudière and removed a slim cigarette case, flicked it open, tapped a cigarette against the metal. "She's making the Fontana sisters an international name."

"Since when do you smoke?"

"I don't. It's all show."

"I don't get it."

"Of course you don't. You're a man."

He smirked. "Need a light with the insult?"

Her shoulder against the wall. "It's not just fashion. It's women looking out for each other. Quietly. But it counts."

Walker looked again at Audrey and Clare. "Is that how it works?"

She shrugged. "When it can. In a world built for men, we find our ways."

Walker studied the two women. "Audrey whispered something in French to me earlier."

"What did she say?"

He tried to repeat it, but mangled it. Leslie grinned, either at the imitation or the message. "She told you to be careful."

"Sarcasm?"

"No. A warning. You were standing next to Dulles. She read you."

"Read me?"

"Like a book. She's not just an actress, Walker. She was a member of the Dutch Resistance."

Clare moved again, this time toward a tall, aquiline man in a dark suit with a coupe glass in hand. His posture was effortless, his expression half-formed amusement. He held his cigarette upright like a conductor's baton.

Leslie stiffened enough for Walker to notice.

"Who's that?"

Through tight teeth: "Luchino Visconti."

Visconti inclined his head in the faintest nod to Luce, cigarette poised in his long fingers.

"I hope you're enjoying Rome, Ambassador."

"I am, thank you. Rome is the Eternal City for good reason."

"Though Americans keep trying to change her."

"We're fond of ruins. We just prefer them rebuilt."

He sipped his drink. "Rebuilt, or repurposed?"

Her answer, smooth as marble. "Beauty rarely survives chaos."

Visconti tilted his head, as if amused she'd accepted the challenge. "Chaos is where beauty begins, Ambassador. Especially in cinema. Or revolution."

"In diplomacy, it tends to end in funerals."

Their eyes met. A détente established between them.

Laughter broke out. Glasses clinked. A pianist instigated gaiety with a Cole Porter song.

Dulles appeared at Walker's elbow. "Time to adjourn," he said. "Dinner awaits."

* * *

The dinner was elegant, as expected. In the private room off the Excelsior's main dining hall, the table was set with china, cut crystal, and a white linen runner that caught the flicker of candlelight. The walls held their heat from the Roman day; the air smelled faintly of lemon and tobacco. A waiter had cleared the *secondo piatto* of veal saltimbocca with sage, as a server set down silverware for dessert.

Seated with her back to the unlit fireplace, posture impeccable, hands folded, eyes sharp behind the courteous smile, Walker sat across from Luce, with Leslie at his side. Dulles, at the head of the table, nursed a Scotch, neat. A dessert of fig tartlets was accompanied by small crystal glasses of Amaro Lucano.

Before Dulles could reply, the door to the room swung open. Kim Roosevelt, suit jacket missing, shirt sleeves wrinkled, hair wind-tossed, entered like a man who'd forgotten his manners, despite his family's name.

He carried no hat, offered no greeting, and made no apology. He strode in, a cowboy, all business and as if he expected accounts settled yesterday.

"I need print materials, translated into Farsi." He dropped into an empty chair, summoned a waiter with a snap of his fingers, and requested a whiskey. The waiter rushed off. The table fell into silence. Dulles's expression remained neutral, but his left hand gripped a napkin.

"Quite the entrance, Kim. Please say hello to Ambassador Luce, and this is Leslie and Walker."

Kim nodded curtly. "Ambassador." Then, to Dulles: "Saidi has stirred things up again. God, he's—he's like a pebble in my damn shoe. We could crush this whole thing with the right pamphlets and speeches. It's how it works, isn't it?"

"Take it up with Walker here, Kim. He's the gentleman you haven't bothered to address, or did you leave your manners behind in Oyster Bay?"

"Point taken, Director. My apologies, Walker." Kim delivered it like a schoolboy prompted by a disapproving headmaster.

Luce spoke, dry but measured. "I'd prefer not to hear the details, for obvious reasons."

The arched eyebrow made it clear she knew the name Saidi.

Kim waved her off, unfazed. "People need something to hold on to. Flyers, editorials, pamphlets—anything that moves them closer to the objective." He finally looked at Walker. "I assume that's your department."

A waiter appeared with whiskey and set it on the linen in front of Kim. Walker asked for Leslie's cigarette case. She handed it to him. He opened the case, removed a cigarette, but didn't light it. Kim neither noticed a lighter nor a match within reach.

A concierge stepped into the room, apologized for the intrusion, and handed Walker a folded telegram. Unmarked, but clearly urgent.

Walker read it once. Folded it. Without inflection, to Kim: "Today is your lucky day."

Dulles's gaze sharpened. Kim pulled his head back. "It is?"

Walker announced as he tapped the cigarette against the metal case:

"You'll have your materials, Kim."

Leslie raised her glass to no one in particular.

"To print runs and plausible deniability."

Chapter Twenty-Seven

Leslie slept. Walker was awake, showered, shaved, dressed, and downstairs. He walked into the quiet bar, his desire for an espresso was visceral. Sunlight poured into the room. The barman anticipated his craving or, satisfying his own, was already at the machine, pulling dark energy into porcelain. It was one of those days when the world felt like it belonged to him—when he woke up early enough and felt as if he could accomplish the Twelve Labors of Hercules by 9 a.m., and then have breakfast.

Walker thanked the man, took the demitasse and saucer, turned—and saw he was not alone. Across the room, at a table in a yellow summer dress, sat Audrey Hepburn. Her large eyes peered over a wide cappuccino. The chair opposite her moved with the groan of wood on marble. She was inviting him to join her. The gesture was subtle, but unmistakable.

"Miss Hepburn."

She smiled. "Audrey, please. Join me, Walker."

He sat down. Everything about her suggested quiet elegance. He'd met Hollywood starlets when he doctored scripts at Warner Brothers, but they were brash, all elbows and ambition. She was different.

"You remembered me?"

"I remember you were with Allen Dulles."

"Faulting me for the company I keep?" he said.

The girlish smile that wasn't girlish. "The operative word is company."

She spoke with a distinct and refined British accent. Leslie had told him that in England, speech betrayed class. She'd added that Americans comforted themselves with the lie that class didn't exist in America.

"About what you said to me in French." He sipped the astringent liquid.

"You can take that without sugar?"

"I drank worse in the war. Even bad coffee was a godsend."

"I cried when I had my first real meal after the war. We lived on nothing."

So poised, so skilled, she didn't leave a trace of lipstick on the rim.

"I was told you were in the resistance."

"My mother was more active. I was a child. I didn't really do anything extraordinary." She said it softly, gently, eyes cast downward.

"The Nazis didn't make distinctions."

Her eyes lifted. She was beautiful. "I know."

"Your advice the other night?"

"Silence is your friend."

A hotel guest approached, apologetic. He wanted an autograph for his daughter. Hepburn didn't refuse. She smiled with warmth and insisted it was no intrusion. She detected something in his voice and switched from Italian to French, then back again. He walked away, clutching a prized piece of paper.

Walker admired her linguistic grace.

"Thank God he was from France, and not from Germany, or Switzerland. My German is terrible."

"You're a modest woman, Audrey. It's endearing."

"Now, don't be a flirt. I don't think you'd want to incur Leslie's wrath."

"She isn't the jealous type."

"You have a lot to learn about women."

"It's the second time I've heard that," Walker said, finishing his espresso.

"Our lessons in life disappear once we learn what we must."

"And Dulles?"

"Dance is my passion, Walker. A teacher once told me melody seduces, but the beat is the truth. Follow that, and you won't lose your step. Not in life, not in love, not even with him."

She rose, placed her hand on his shoulder, and he held it for a long second. And then she was gone.

***

Leslie sat at the vanity, hair wet. Her eyes caught him in the mirror when he walked into the room. A brush moved slowly through dark hair as she watched him.

"Morning," she said. Cool and calm, the kind before and after a battle.

He sensed it immediately—the edge of suspicion in her tone.

"*Buongiorno*. I needed coffee and couldn't wait," he said.

"*Bonjour*." The hairbrush pushed through a knot.

"This is Italy. Why the French?"

The brush clattered. She didn't turn away from her own reflection.

"Audrey spoke French to you the other night," she said. "So I counted on consistency."

"She speaks Italian well, too. How did you know?"

"Dulles called while you were out."

His eyebrows shot up. "Man has eyes everywhere. What did he say?"

"You two are to enjoy a day trip."

"Say where?"

She rose, cinched the sash of her robe. Her voice was clipped. Her accent bled through.

"No, and why would he tell me?" She went to walk past him. He grabbed her, spun her so that she faced him. Her hand pressed against his chest. He leaned in for a kiss.

He felt her nails through his shirt.

"Not a good idea, Walker."

"Why not?"

"I'm many things, but I'm still a woman."

Not retreating, she claimed her space in the room.

"What the hell does that mean?"

Halfway to the bathroom, she turned around. "I'd rather you think of me, not Audrey."

The door to the bathroom slammed shut. Solid oak, pre-war construction. The kind that muffled things you didn't want to hear.

He stared at the door. Nothing moved.

* * *

Walker stepped out to get some fresh air and to allow Leslie time to herself. It seemed hotter inside the Excelsior than outside.

He returned to find his linen suit and shirt pressed and laid out on the bed. Shoes at the foot of the bed. He frowned. Odd gesture of peace, he thought. He heard water running in the bathroom. She emerged, fixing an earring.

"What's this?" He looked at the ensemble.

"What does it look like?

"I'm a grown man who doesn't need a mother dressing him."

She stepped closer, her arms behind her, busy.

"No, but you're still a schoolboy when you consider the company you'll have later."

His mind flashed back to Audrey earlier. "Company, meaning Dulles."

"And someone else," she said. Her skirt dropped to the floor. "My guess is Andreotti."

"I see," he said, his words deliberate and ambiguous. "Where did you go while I was out?"

"To Villa Taverna."

"To see Clare?"

"She is unwell."

It was common knowledge that more people caught the flu during the summer than any other season, or suffered from hay fever. Then he remembered the earlier bit about Clare thinking she was being poisoned. That was his hasty diagnosis while he watched Leslie unbutton the front of her blouse, one button at a time.

"Is she okay?"

"Time will tell. Symptoms include fatigue, headaches, and nausea. She says her hair has started to fall out. The first two I attribute to overwork, the third to her eating like a bird, and the fourth to vanity." She parted the blouse. "Then again, I'm no doctor." She peeled off the blouse.

"Could be the summer heat."

"Could be."

She stepped closer. Her eyes met his.

She unhooked her bra. "How 'bout you finish that thought you had this morning."

* * *

Walker kept to the military habit of arriving at least ten minutes early for an appointment. He stood outside the Excelsior. Dulles appeared in a tan linen suit, pressed, straw fedora low, American-style sunglasses, sharp and angular. A black Chrysler Imperial pulled up. The driver was unfamiliar. The doorman opened the rear door. Dulles nodded, "You first."

Walker stepped inside. Dulles joined him. The door clapped shut, and the car pulled away. Not a word was said to the driver. He knew their destination.

Walker watched the streets. Dulles checked his watch. The Company's Director looked preoccupied—as if, briefly, a human heart beat inside the cold warrior. Walker remembered Audrey's advice: *Silence is your friend.*

"We should be there in thirty to forty minutes," Dulles said.

Walker didn't ask where or why. Military training had taught him: if it mattered, they'd tell you. A sign passed by: Via Cristoforo Colombo. Southbound. Nineteen miles to an American, thirty kilometers to everyone else.

Dulles broke the silence. "Audrey is lovely, isn't she?"

Walker waited, cautious. The cocktail hour—or that morning?

"A kind woman. Lovely."

"The kindest people," Dulles said, "have usually seen cruelty."

"Sir?"

"I'd add the funniest, too."

"As in comedians?"

"Genuine wit requires intelligence. Sarcasm anyone can do."

"I hadn't thought of it that way."

"Actors make for wonderful agents."

Walker tested the waters. "Because they wear a mask?"

"No. Because many of them don't know who they are to begin with." Dulles looked out the window as he said it.

The remark floated for a moment—neutral on the surface, but heavy underneath.

Walker nodded. "Someone should recruit Miss Hepburn, then."

Dulles smiled. "Who says no one has?"

More road passed. A sign read Torvaianica.

"That beach," Dulles said, "draws the wrong sort of attention these days."

"Sir?"

"In April, before you arrived, a young woman—Wilma Montesi—was found dead there. Twenty-one. Suicide, some say. Others say not. Beautiful, from a good family."

He adjusted his cufflink. For a moment, he looked like a man who cared. "The newspapers lit up. Some say to divert attention from the *Balena bianca*. That's white whale, in Italian."

"White whale?"

"The Christian Democrats. The '48 election was hard work, and we're not letting a scandal with sex, drugs, and a body on a beach sink our investment."

Walker understood the implication. Andreotti, as Interior Minister, kept it contained.

The car slowed. A modest *pensione* near the sea. A sun-bleached umbrella sat outside like a signal. Walker scanned the area: a faded Fiat, a priest who wasn't a priest smoked a cigarette against a stucco wall. Dulles's door opened and shut behind him.

Inside, a barkeep wiped the counter without looking up. Dulles walked straight through.

In the back room: a table, a pitcher of *acqua frizzante*, and Giulio Andreotti in dark summer-weight wool, like a Roman cleric would wear. He stood and greeted Dulles, who introduced Walker.

"You were behind Director Dulles," Andreotti said with a half-smile.

They sat. Andreotti sipped an iced espresso. Dulles took off his sunglasses.

"I'll get to the point."

"Simplicity is sophistication."

"Signs suggest arsenic. Villa Taverna."

Andreotti's brow barely moved. "It was built before the war, though walls never forget. Your theory?"

"Soviets. Or someone inside your party." Dulles opened and closed his hands slowly, like a clamshell. "Poison isn't always meant to kill. Sometimes it just sends a message." He paused. "If it was meant to kill, it failed. If it wasn't, then it's just begun."

Andreotti took this in. "And the message?"

"Our people are not safe in Rome. That's a message we cannot let stand."

"And what is it you think I can do for you, Director?"

Dulles poured a glass of water. It fizzed.

"You know every pair of shoes that walks through the capital."

Walker stayed silent. He wasn't just watching. He weighed words. This wasn't about one poisoned diplomat. This was a signal flare, uncertain in direction, certain in intent.

"Walker's here because we've begun something. He's my man."

Dulles tapped his glass—once. Twice. A third time. Like a pulse.

Andreotti noticed. "You're worried about water?"

"It drowns; it puts out fires."

"Oil burns," Andreotti said. "And I'm concerned about British fingerprints."

The tapping stopped.

"I'll ensure there are no prints," Dulles said, "if you do the same."

Andreotti leaned in. "You'll have my help in Rome, if Mattei remains untouched in Persia."

Now it came into focus. Tasked with dismantling Mussolini's oil infrastructure and replacing it with one of his own, Mattei was negotiating deals in the Middle East and undercutting the Anglo-Iranian monopoly. Mosaddegh in Tehran had a similar plan. The British hated them both.

Two fronts. One fire. Whoever controlled the oil, controlled winter.

Andreotti stood. So did Dulles. They shook hands.

A breeze came through the narrow back window.

Cool, salted, and laced with cigarette smoke.

The priest was gone.

Chapter Twenty-Eight

The Imperial slipped away behind them, a trace of exhaust curling in the dying summer light. Evening would soon fall, and night would begin the second act. It was the hours between midnight and dawn that determined life and death. Walker knew it.

A doorman held the door.

"A drink, shall we?" Dulles said.

More statement than question. Walker said nothing.

He glanced over his shoulder for one last glimpse of the world outside, then followed Dulles inside.

Hotels were not home; they became havens. Dulles called the Excelsior his second office. Whether he spun the rotary dial in D.C. or Rome, the call reached ears. He made the world small.

They walked to the back of the bar. Dulles flashed two fingers at the barman.

He set his straw fedora on the chair beside him, unbuttoned his jacket, and sat. Walker mirrored him. The ritual of deference. The barkeep arrived with two whiskeys. Dulles thanked him and waited. Blue eyes met blue eyes—similar in color, worlds apart.

Dulles pretend-smiled. "You did well."

Walker had kept his vow of silence on the drive back from Ostia, suppressing the urge to speak or scream.

He looked down. Dulles already had fingers curled around the glass.

The congratulations was not the toast. That might come later. Or not at all. Dulles wasn't Jack. He didn't toss drinks back. Everything in its time, like Ecclesiastes.

"It's my understanding you and Jack shared a drink after assignments. True?"

"Yes."

Dulles looked down, then back up, smiling. "Never say Yes or No."

"Sir?"

"To cast the affirmative or negative closes every door. Ends the scene. You should know that from writing scripts at Warner Brothers."

"I learned fast as I could because I wasn't a writer."

"You came to writing late. That makes you better."

"You mean, because of life experience?"

"No. I mean patience and an appreciation for craft. You weren't one of those who declared yourself a writer at five, crayon in hand."

"Some people don't find their way, Sir."

"And some write like they still hold crayons. Your time in Hollywood taught you character on the page. You already understood character from life."

"I did?"

"You listened. Foremost virtue of a writer. Observation is intel."

Walker held his glass. Dulles recast the initial question.

"If you don't answer Yes or No, what do you say instead?"

Walker leaned back. A retest. He noticed the stillness in Dulles' fingers. Nothing about this man was idle. "I'd say either, 'On occasion, why?' or 'First time I've heard that about me and Jack.'"

Dulles smiled. "Excellent. Plausible deniability. One response hints but doesn't confirm. The other forces doubt in the questioner's source. Simple, but not simple."

Walker leaned forward, as a subtle shift, quiet pressure. "That kind of dialogue works in a movie. In real life, a question to a question earns you a punch in the nose."

"Thought editors used a blue pencil, not red?"

The smile said he'd led Walker onto the killing floor.

"Some do, some don't."

"No, Walker. A teacher uses red to signal error—distress. An editor uses blue because it vanishes during reproduction. Camouflage. Dramatic red versus subtle blue."

Walker tapped his temple. "I salute you, sir. You ambushed me."

"I lured you. Conversation as combat."

"And Jack's telegram, the conversation earlier?"

"We met Andreotti because of an unexpected development."

Walker said, "An ill ambassador isn't a small bump in the road."

"A dead diplomat is." Dulles paused. "Jack's asset secured use of the Xerox machines in Tehran. As you put it at the soirée with Kim at the table—Kim's lucky day. Jack delivered."

"About Kim." Walker's finger tapped the glass.

"Don't worry about him."

"Jack taught me never to underestimate anyone."

"Including me?" Dulles smiled, enjoying the foreplay.

"Especially you. But before I ask my question—a personal one."

Dulles nodded. "Ask it."

"How is Clare?"

"The navy doctor confirmed arsenic. She'll recover."

"Good. And Kim?"

"You're the writer, Walker. Define his character for me."

"Brash. Impulsive. A touch maniacal. Whether that's good or bad depends on the scene."

"Excellent," Dulles said. "Context. Circumstance. Those two inform the scene, drive action, and we're in the business of creation. You have a scene, a decision. Choose the weapon."

"A person as a weapon?"

"Kim is a bull in a porcelain shop. In combat, you either put a man like him up front, to inspire or burn out, or in the rear to mop up. Both valid. Context, again."

Walker studied Dulles. A man of calculus, not conscience. Truman had warned him. Dulles read names and numbers on the Killed List. He didn't see, nor wanted to see, the Gold Star mother or the casket lowered into the ground at Arlington. Profits and Losses, this was an accountant of death.

"And Norman in Tehran?"

"You were there with Andreotti."

"He'll help find the poisoners, in exchange for what he wants."

"With a bull, you need the horns."

"Andreotti is no bull."

"I wasn't talking about Andreotti."

"You mean Kim?"

"Orient the bull. The horns do the rest."

"Kim and Norman are very different bulls."

"Same result," Dulles said. "Few know that, in a bullfight, the animal's nostrils are stuffed with rags dipped in blood. He's enraged by instinct—the blood—and driven by necessity—he can't breathe."

Dulles was writing the scene.

"And I'd like to know a character's motivation, so the scene works."

"Know Latin?"

"Not well. But Andreotti would."

"Ad majorem Dei gloriam inque hominum salute."

Walker waited.

"For the greater glory of God and the salvation of humanity," Dulles said. "But in this corrupted world, it becomes motivation, as in the greater glory of Kim."

"And humanity in your quote?"

"That's Norman—and the British belief they're everyone's superior."

Dulles looked into him.

"Ever wonder why I picked you, Walker? You're not Ivy League. Your German is atrocious."

"You know how to punch and flatter in the same breath."

"If you're perfect on the page, you're not perfect."

"Excuse me?"

"Leslie's better at languages. Norman's fluent in Farsi. Too fluent. Too close to the water. That's why MI6 has him in Tehran. Perfectionism is deadly. Moral ambition, lethal."

Walker felt the room shift. Like Dulles had tilted the floor beneath him.

"You don't speak German well. Leslie does. Doesn't matter. The locals already know you're the outsider. Speak enough to get by. Don't try to be British. Norman speaks like a native, but one look, and they know he's British."

"And me? I'm the objective one?"

"You are the matador. You control the bulls. And the horns."

"If Norman is British and blinkered, he's compromised. He may hesitate."

Dulles said nothing. He didn't need to.

"Kim won't hesitate."

"We don't need Kim to squeeze the trigger. We need him to deliver the documents and money. Jack's asset made the Xerox machines possible. Kim's ego will do the rest."

Walker saw the scene come into focus: machines, leaflets, the war of persuasion.

"I thought Norman was writing the content. In Farsi."

Dulles shook his head. "No."

"Didn't you say 'No' closes doors?"

"If any door closes, it's on the British. I have someone in New York—Bernays and translators—already at work. It'll arrive by diplomatic pouch by week's end. You will hand it to Kim."

"And he delivers it to the Xerox machines?"

"Correct."

"And Norman?"

"He accepts what comes off the press."

"No red pen or blue pencil?"

"Not a chance."

Walker heard it for what it was—strategy wrapped in dialogue. Consent without choice.

"And Saidi?" he asked. "Is he Kim's or Norman's problem?"

"No. He is yours."

Saidi was the man Kim called a 'pebble in his shoe,' a potential threat.

"Norman's in Tehran." Walker blinked. "He's the best man to make that call."

"A decision. But the decision is yours."

Walker heard the distinction, the articles in his sentence.

Dulles let it hang—not an order, not even a suggestion. A test.

"There's another reason Norman isn't objective."

Dulles explained the death of Mahmoud Afshartous—abducted, tortured, killed, days after Wilma Montesi in Ostia. Norman believed he could flip Afshartous. MI6 couldn't wait. They acted. Preemptive, like Kim would.

"You think Saidi's another Afshartous?"

Dulles didn't answer. He raised his glass.

Chapter Twenty-Nine

Exhausted, like the day he'd run his personal best. 'Three Miles Up, Three Miles Down.' His face red as Georgia mud. The heat. The humidity. Mosquitoes and misery. Walker approached his hotel room, dreaming of a bed, when he heard voices on the other side of the door.

A woman and a man. Leslie, defensive. The man: unmistakably British.

He jingled his keys, deliberately loud, and entered.

Not quite the stare of Bambi in the woods, but close.

"I'm too annoyed to care," Walker said, "but what the hell is this?"

He shut the door. No one spoke. A moment ago, voices had been raised. Controlled, clipped, British. Leslie sounded like London itself: furious, but not from Adolf's bombs.

The man he saw now was the man behind them at the lake. MI6.

It clicked. The Home Office had sent someone to 'have a word.' Leslie wasn't having it.

Walker peeled off his jacket, hooked it on a chair.

Leslie stepped toward the credenza and picked up a cigarette from a crystal tray. She turned it in her fingers but didn't light it. A gesture, nothing more.

"Someone care to speak?" Walker asked, sounding like a disappointed headmaster.

"No need for the tone," the man said.

"Nice try for the upper hand. But this is Rome. Not London."

"And now you're acting like a boss. When we met on the road, she drove."

That she'd driven, not Walker, was meant as a dig.

"Sometimes women are the better driver. Care to give a name?"

"Miles Meersby, not your service."

Walker glanced to Leslie. "I can see why you joined us."

"And what's that supposed to mean?"

Walker stepped closer. "Name's alliterative. Just enough to make Maugham stutter. You do know he was SIS, don't you?"

"Of course. That was ages ago. What's that got to do with anything?"

"That was then. This is now. Leslie's with us." A look to her. "Unless you've changed your mind."

She exhaled slowly. "Not a chance."

"And no possibility you're playing both sides? Miles looks the sentimental type."

Miles bristled. "And what does that make you?"

"A realist." Walker's stance shifted. "Step back before I offer you breath fresheners and a fist."

Miles stood at attention, hands behind his back.

"What's your business here, Miles?"

"To talk to the lady."

"Oh, now she's a lady. The noise I heard suggested otherwise. If this was all above board, why not an office or a café? Why here?"

"I wanted to know where she stood."

"With you, or with MI6?"

His eyes narrowed. "Strictly professional. There was never anything between us."

"How about between her and Ajax?"

"Come again?"

"Let's go big and bold. We call it Ajax. What does the Home Office call it?"

"Boot, if you must know."

"I must. You're here because you're worried we stripped the British out like old wiring."

Miles scoffed. "We were in Persia long before you showed up. It will remain ours. The wiring still carries current."

"Like it does in India?"

The jab landed.

Leslie's voice cut in. "You've made your point, Walker."

"You're right." He lifted his jacket off the chair and walked it to the armoire. "It's been a long day."

Miles said, "Enjoy Ostia?"

"I did. It was educational. Let me guess—the barkeep?"

Miles didn't answer. The question implied that the bartender was MI6's plant.

Walker thought of Ostia again, the two drinks and two men at the table. Andreotti and Dulles drew lines without raising voices. They were calm, cool, detached. The room here was warmer, tighter, and the war was personal.

"I'll have materials for Norman. They'll arrive in person, via Kim."

Surprise registered in his eyes. "Him?"

Walker's smile was thin. "Yes. Kim Roosevelt."

"Oh bloody hell. I'd prefer Christ on a donkey to that man flipping tables at the temple. I get that you Americans lust for results, but a little finesse wouldn't kill you."

"We're young at empire," Walker said. "We're babes. And babies' teeth."

Miles stepped to the door. "Days, you said?"

"By week's end."

Hand on the knob, Meersby stopped. "I'll let Darbyshire know the good news."

He left. The door clicked shut. Polite, surgical.

Walker leaned against the wall. Silence.

Leslie didn't move. "He's not wrong," she said. "About finesse."

Walker nodded once. "We all bleed different shades of empire."

The light in the room turned amber as the sun finally dropped.

Chapter Thirty

Tania watched.

Esther Pomerantz lounged on the other side of the pool, surrounded by her usual coterie. Tania observed her through a pair of men's sunglasses, Ray-Bans. The cool smoke-gray lenses she would tell you kept her steady, detached, and clinical. The Vuarnets with green glass she'd given Ruth were for clarity. If children viewed the world through kaleidoscopes when they played, Tania used different colored lenses as filters to bring shades of truth into sharp focus.

Tania reclined in a poolside chair, Judith on her left, Ruth on her right. Across the pool, Esther sat posed wearing white sunglasses, in a one-piece suit and a wrap around her hips. Her girls giggled too often, too loud. One carried the latest magazines, another held a metal caddy of Coca-Colas.

Judith spoke. "She knows you're watching."

"Good," Tania said.

Since the 'L Incident'—that cruel prank involving a drink and an unwanted surprise — Judith had become invisible in the worst way. No one needed to explain what the L stood for. Her emergence from the restroom, her pale appearance, fueled gossip. There were stares from other kids. Whispers. Pity from older women. And then came the cruel reminders: a sheet of toilet paper or a whole roll left near her things or on her chair. A Little Tree air freshener shaped like a Christmas tree was an irony not lost on anyone.

Judith said she wanted revenge, then said forget it. Tania would not let it be forgotten.

Ruth pestered her, now in a whisper. "When? When do we do something?"

"In the fullness of time."

"What are you waiting for?"

"A pattern. A tell."

"A tell?"

"A weakness."

Across the water, Esther adjusted the strap of her bathing suit. Every movement was calculated, down to the flick of her wrist. Tania catalogued all of it, from the way Esther never fully stretched her legs, how she kept her arms tight to her sides, or the quiet touch she gave one girl—Rachel something—just above the elbow, precise as dotting an 'i' in a sentence. Not strange. Not overt. But something.

Her smile showed teeth, but there was nothing behind it. No warmth. No true connection.

Ruth murmured, "Is it wrong, wanting revenge?"

Tania didn't answer at first.

"Aren't we supposed to forgive?"

"That's 'turn the other cheek.' This world lives by the Old Testament."

"Are you religious?"

"No. But if the Bible shaped civilization, I want to understand the world it left behind."

Judith listened, said nothing. Tania turned toward Ruth, serious now.

"The world is full of patterns. We're all different, but we're also the same. We're instinctual. We pick up on signals and differences, even if we don't fully understand them. At some point, the world singled out being Jewish as 'different,' and that difference came with a heavy cost—one that forgiveness couldn't erase. Once you're marked like that, it's no longer about forgiveness. It becomes a matter of survival."

"Are you saying we deserved it—if we don't stop them, it'll happen again?"

"History books seem to say that is the case."

Tania leaned back again, eyes on Esther, who now lay on her stomach, chin on folded arms. Her laughter was high and artificial and drifted over the water like the chlorine in the pool. A boy passed. One of her girls whispered. More giggles. Esther didn't look at him.

Tania noticed.

She noticed everything.

Later, in the resort library, she found the sign-out sheet. Esther had been there, the handwriting careful, feminine. A Radclyffe Hall novel. A few days before, *To the Lighthouse* had disappeared. No one would notice. Tania did.

Judith adjusted her towel. "People talk, you know."

"They always do."

"They talk about you, Tania."

"I don't care."

"It doesn't help if you give them material."

"I can't change that I'm the *shiksa*. Or *meshuggah*."

Judith hesitated. "The lottery is later this week."

Tania tried levity. "Does that mean everyone gets a copy of Shirley Jackson?"

The joke fell flat. But they were friends. It didn't need to land.

The lottery. July gone. August present. Esther's slot in the show assured, trophy and cash prize assumed because her father would see to it.

"She wants to win bad," Judith said.

"I know."

"Her father'll rig it."

"Like Rothstein and the World Series. I'm counting on it."

Esther was an easy target. Tania had handled worse.

She remembered the cabin, also in upstate New York. The man Roy Cohn sent. The floorboards. What came after. How it ended.

She remembered the look in the man's eyes before she pulled the trigger.

Judith again. "What if your name is in the lottery?"

"What if it is?"

"It would be so like Esther to have your name show up, so she can humiliate you, like she did with me."

"I'm not you, Judith."

The remark registered, might've stung. Judith asked anyway. "Got any talents?"

Tania smiled, slow and careful.

"I might."

Chapter Thirty-One

Time crawled, as summer days are meant to.

These were the days meant for memory and nostalgia in old age, when the look over the shoulder revealed a world simpler than the one at the end. The past always looks simpler, but it never is or was.

Tania had never known innocence. But she knew this moment mattered, and gave herself permission to enjoy it. She walked barefoot through grass. There was a time when she walked over cinders, stepped over rubble, and dead bodies. That was lifetimes ago. It didn't mean she had forgotten all that had brought her to this present moment. Images lingered, the odors of decay and death haunted her.

She saw Judith in the distance in front of the Activities Board.

Judith sensed her, turned, and smiled.

They both read the large chalkboard together.

"Mrs. Finklestein is sure organized." Admiration in Judith's voice. "She wrote this before services."

Tania was reading down the list when Judith did something unexpected. She put her arm around Tania's waist. It was an unexpected gesture, human touch unlike what she had experienced.

August 16, 1953: Sunday Schedule
    10:00 AM: Archery Practice (North Lawn)
    11:30 AM: Rehearsals (Location at Your Leisure)
    1:00 PM: Lunch (Main Dining Room)
    2:30 PM: Canoe Races (Dock)

4:00 PM: Song Circle & Root Beer Floats (Main Dining Room)
7:00 PM: Talent Show (Rec Hall)
TBD: Bonfire (South Lawn)

"Mrs. Finklestein didn't write this," Tania said.

Judith looked to the board, then to Tania. "If not her, then who?"

"Esther. I recognize the handwriting."

"How do you know and why?"

"Dunno why, but it's Esther's cursive. I've seen it."

Tania left it at that and didn't elaborate further. Esther's cursive wasn't the bland Palmer Method taught in schools. Like most teenagers, she tried to assert a style that she could call her own. It strived for a masculine boldness yet remained feminine and fancy. It made sense to Tania, aligned with her hypothesis of Judith struggling to write her own *Bildungsroman*.

Tania considered herself blessed to know who and what she was, even if the metamorphosis was painful. Christ had harrowed hell in the three days he was dead, and Tania thought of herself as one of those left behind and forgotten. She had found her way to the surface, a pagan and without Orpheus or the sound of music to guide her to the land of the living.

Judith rested her head against Tania's. "Do you have a shawl?"

"It's summer, Judy. Why would I need a shawl?"

"Services. You need to cover your head."

Tania hadn't expected this. "I haven't attended any of the services, so why now?"

"Because I'm inviting you, and because Sheldon was asked to recite the Mourner's Kaddish. If not for me, you should attend for him; it's a big deal. People have seen the numbers on his arm. They know, so they asked him."

"I will," she said.

"On a lighter note, the lottery drawing is after Shabbat ends."

* * *

Kids thirteen years of age and older were eligible for the Talent Show. They rehearsed their acts all summer, each uncertain whether their name would be drawn. Some hoped for the best: if chosen, they would perform their best. If not, the year could be spent honing their act for next season.

Tania passed by several performances across the resort grounds. Marty Rabinowitz and Saul Levy were in the middle of a chaotic comedy sketch about a circumcision gone wrong, their voices an exaggerated mix of Jackie Mason and Henny Youngman. It was ridiculous, borderline offensive, but undeniably hilarious. A few boys imitated vaudeville acts, such as Milton Berle and the Marx Brothers, while the bolder ones attempted song-and-dance numbers. Most were passable, but none had that raw, unpolished spark of something great.

The girls, in contrast, stuck with the conservative. Piano recitals. Sweet, uneventful songs. No surprises. Tania had hoped for the physical comedy of a Gracie Allen, or the sultry allure of a Hedy Lamarr. Instead, she saw timid performances, the kind that didn't even strain for originality. They lacked the guts. *Chutzpah.*

Mrs. Geller roved the grounds, doling out advice in sharp, staccato bursts.

"Girls, save the lipstick for after practice."

"Stand tall, Sidney. No one wants Quasimodo."

"Ballerinas sweat. Dance like you mean it."

"*Im Yishem.* Squirrels in saddle shoes dance better."

Tania heard it and had to ask Judith for a translation. 'God help me.'

Judith had her own question to ask of Tania. "Have you practiced, just in case?"

Tania gave a slow smile. "I know exactly what I'm doing."

* * *

The shawl borrowed from Judith draped over her head and shoulders. Tania watched Sheldon from the corner of her eye, feeling the soft dance of light from the Shabbat candles catch something in his face. It wasn't the usual mask of detachment. There was something older, heavier there, as if the sum of all his memories had caught up with him. His gaze seemed distant,

153

like a man out of place in time, his eyes on something unseen, perhaps the ghosts of the past.

The rabbi made the introduction. Sheldon stepped forward, his movements slow, deliberate. His fingers fidgeted with the cuff of his shirt, as though trying to ground himself in the present moment. People whispered, but soon silence became absolute, the air thick with anticipation. Sheldon was the eye of this storm—the center of both history and memory.

He began, his voice soft but clear. The words of the Mourner's Kaddish spilled from him like a familiar refrain, each one a small, calculated release of tension.

"Yit'gadal v'yit'kadash sh'mei raba…"

There was nothing particularly strained in his delivery. Words carried weight—his voice steady with an emotional restraint, of holding back something deeper.

The phrases, though familiar to the congregation, now felt different. These were not words of praise; they were prayers for those lost. But to Sheldon, they were not merely about the dead; they were about the survivors like himself, about wounds that never healed, and shattered lives. Each word was a burden from lives torn apart, a thousand broken pieces sewn back together in a way that would never be whole.

As he continued, the silence stretched tight but didn't break. The weight of his grief was not in the words of the prayer but in the spaces between them. His eyes never left the small cluster of candles in front of him, as though he were searching for something only they could reveal.

"Oseh shalom bimromav, hu ya'aseh shalom aleinu…"

His voice quivered slightly on the last syllable, but it did not falter. The prayer did not rush; it lingered in the air, heavy with the lives he had lost—and those he had failed to save.

The Kaddish ended, but Sheldon's presence filled the room, as if he had pulled the ghosts of the past into the present. A stillness that resonated through the room. But for a brief moment, the past had been alive in him, and they had all felt it.

The rabbi's voice, gentle and respectful, broke the silence.

"Thank you, Sheldon. You honor the dead."

Sheldon gave a slight nod. It was as though he hadn't heard the rabbi at all. His eyes were unfocused, as if he were already somewhere else, his mind wandering through memories he had no intention of sharing.

He retreated to the back, into the shadows, his mask back in place. The Sheldon Tania knew had returned, composed and detached.

Chapter Thirty-Two

In the Main Dining Room, Mr. Finkelstein stood by the dessert table and called out in his best Catskills cadence.

"Ladies and gentlemen, I hope you've all had a restful Shabbos. And now, for something a little more upbeat. As you know, tomorrow evening is the annual Talent Show, and because we have so many brilliant young people, we have to draw names to limit the number of contestants. Before my lovely wife draws the first name from this punch bowl—which, I assure you, has been thoroughly cleaned—I just want to say: *mazel tov.*"

Ripples of anticipation moved through the room. A few kids sat up straighter. Some parents leaned forward.

"Esther Klein," Mrs. Finkelstein announced first.

Esther Pomerantz flinched, ready to pounce, then sat back. False alarm.

Then came Judith Weissman. A few more names followed.

And then: "Esther Pomerantz."

Predictable. If ping-pong balls had been used, Tania might have suspected sinkers, weighted just enough to make Esther's name float to the top.

"Last but not least," Mrs. Finkelstein said, lifting one final slip from the bowl. "Tania."

A murmur of surprise moved across the room. Esther and Tania locked eyes.

Then a voice cut through the tension.

"News from the Middle East." An unexpected distraction.

It was Isaac Feldman, or Ike as everyone called him. Nerd to most, genius to a few.

Tania saw Sheldon's eyes widen. He was listening.

Sheldon and a few men followed Ike out toward his makeshift 'laboratory.' Tania followed, Judith and Ruth trailing behind.

Near the ham radio, Ike's cousin Dave was taking notes in pencil, fluent in Hebrew after a year on a kibbutz.

Ike asked, "Anything new?"

One of the men asked, "What are you two listening to?"

"Kol Yisrael," Dave said. "Jerusalem."

Ike put on his headset. Dave kept one earpiece lifted to field questions, the other pressed to listen.

"They're talking about Iran."

"Persia?"

"It's garbled, but sounds like there's been an insurrection."

"A coup?" someone asked.

Dave leaned closer. "Something about the Shah. It's unclear where he is. There's been violence in the streets. Military loyalists. It sounds like the coup failed."

The men began drifting away.

Tania stayed behind, Judith and Ruth with her. Sheldon didn't move. He kept his eyes fixed on the voice coming through the static. Somber.

Chapter Thirty-Three

Several strategically placed fans moved the air in the Main Dining Room, which had been transformed into a makeshift theatre. There was a stage, curtains, lights, performers, and an audience. The air, stirred but still heavy with sweat and perfume. The velvet curtains smelled faintly of dust and mildew, like something stored too long in memory.

Outside, the darkness was so fierce nothing was visible—nothing except the occasional flare of a firefly, seen and then disappeared.

Humdrum acts preceded Esther's, and Tania was the last act of the evening.

Judith took it as a slight. Tania was a Gentile, and no one expected much from her. Ruth, watching her with a more generous eye, thought Tania's stoicism was a front. The girl had a sense of humor; she'd riffed earlier on a line from Dylan Thomas: "Gentiles do not go gentle into that good night."

Arthur Finklestein emceed. When he called her name, the applause for Esther Pomerantz was polite but far from enthusiastic. It wasn't that everyone knew she had laced Judith's drink with laxatives. They did. They clapped because they resented the obvious, that her father had asserted his influence, and nobody likes a blatant display of power.

Esther, always one to command attention, swept onto the stage. The spotlight cast sharp shadows across her features. The rustle of programs. The room quieted as if on cue. Her dress was a perfect replica of Marilyn Monroe's iconic pink one from *Gentlemen Prefer Blondes*, hugging every curve, the thin straps gliding down her shoulders like something out of a dream. Another reason the audience was lukewarm: how convenient that she had brought that dress to the Catskills when everyone else had selected their costumes from the resort's inventory in Storage.

The music started. The beat familiar. The crowd hummed along. There was a ragtag orchestra—geriatric but competent. Leonard Saperstein was no Bernstein, but he commanded his militia with a stern baton. The brass section swelled. Esther took a breath, smiled, and put the number into gear.

Her voice rang out, full of charm and practiced poise.

She stepped lightly, moving across the stage in that exaggerated, theatrical way everyone had seen countless times in films. The performance was polished, brimming with the contradiction of innocence mixed with sexuality. Every movement was graceful, seductive, and designed to make them admire her, to want her. But anyone watching closely could see it was all artifice. Esther offered the illusion of sex. It was camp. It was cinema. The exaggerated lines and movements told a different story: virginity disguised as desire.

Her voice floated in the circulated air, sharp but smooth like honey dripped from a spoon. She sang, head tilted slightly, intent on the men in the front row as if to say: *This is for you, gentlemen.*

The dress. The silk in her voice. The way she moved. She wore the song like a second skin. It was sex she tried to sell, but what she revealed to the audience was that she wanted power, or what her father had as a man, and she lacked as a woman.

Not yet. But someday.

The applause, when it came, was thin and nervous, like everyone had agreed to clap at the same time without quite knowing why. No boos, no cheers. Just sound, and then quiet. An old woman in the second row muttered something in Yiddish that made the woman next to her purse her lips. A teenage boy in the back stared at the stage, visibly confused.

Esther exited stage left, her lips curling in the slightest of smiles. She had nailed it, and she knew it. But something tugged at her—a flicker of doubt she pushed down with the same force she'd once used to crush letters into a fireplace.

She didn't need their applause. She needed their envy. That was the only way women won.

The act that preceded Tania was two young men who thought of themselves as the new Abbott and Costello. Their skit was the classic wordplay, Borscht Belt humor with the tip of the hat to vaudeville. Moishe was the diner at the table, and Abe, his waiter.

"I'm Abe, and I'll be your waiter this evening."

"Alright, I'll try the brisket."

"Excellent choice. With *tzimmes?*"

"What's *tzimmes?*"

"Carrots, sweet potatoes, slow-cooked, very soft. It's a delicious side."

"I don't want a side, I want the brisket."

"But the brisket comes with the side."

"I don't want the side."

"You don't want the *tzimmes?*"

"I don't want to make a *tzimmes.* I want to eat."

"No need to be rude. I heard you twice the first time. You don't want *tzimmes.* Fine. I'll tell the chef to make a *shanda* instead."

"Never mind. Bring me a bagel. Plain. That's it."

Abe scribbled the order on his pad.

"Lox?"

"Don't lock my bagel. I want to eat it, not store it in a safe."

"I meant lox. With salmon."

"You're putting fish on my bagel now?"

"That's what lox is."

"I thought you said lock."

"*Oy vey*, this guy came straight from the Bronx Zoo."

"No lox for you. *Schmear?*"

"Excuse me?"

"Schmear."

"Are you threatening me?"

"It's cream cheese."

"You're gonna smear me now?"

"*Schmear* the bagel."

"Don't you dare touch me."

"Look, mister, either you take the *tzimmes*, the lox, and the *schmear*, or I'll call security."

"Oh, now you're calling the cops over a bagel?"

"I'll get you locked up with the lox."

"And smeared with the *schmear!*"

"And we'll make a whole *tzimmes* out of it."

Moishe sighed. "Alright, fine. Give me the bagel. No lox. No *schmear*."

Applause, whistles. The older folks loved it. Even the teens, rolling their eyes, clapped along.

Esther sat at a table not far from the stage as the lights dimmed for Tania.

Tania had not told the emcee or anyone else what she would perform. She let them wait, made them think she had second thoughts. If Esther's entrance had been primed for applause, Tania's received indifference, like the last kid picked in gym class. The audience waited. Polite. Curious.

And waited.

She walked to center stage, head high. There was a roll of whispers. The *shiksa*. The Gentile. She wore no smile. No sparkle. She wore a tuxedo, borrowed from Storage, tailored by Sheldon. It fit like a black glove. Her blonde hair was slicked back, dyed platinum, and precise. It caught the light like ice.

Her eyes betrayed nothing as she adjusted the microphone.

Tania wasn't here to impress.

She was here for revenge.

The band began. A few notes. The melody familiar, but not.

The crowd shifted, uncomfortable.

She sang the first verse in German, her voice fluid, controlled. The intonation perfect, because she spoke the language. Some caught snippets through Yiddish roots—others stiffened at the sound. A man in the third row leaned back, arms crossed. A woman two seats down whispered, "Is that German?" and didn't wait for an answer.

She switched to English.

Falling in love again, never wanted to.

What am I to do? I can't help it...

Her eyes locked on Esther. Esther's hand went to her throat to touch a necklace that wasn't there.

The performance unfolded.

Tania stepped down into the crowd. She wasn't flirting. She was dismantling. Her voice like velvet over glass. She moved with the cool authority of someone with nothing left to lose.

The second verse. Her eyes never left Esther's.

The music slowed. Tania dipped down—close, closer. She reached out, lifted Esther's chin. Moved in. Her lips near Esther's cheek.

Then—the kiss.

Not erotic. Deliberate. Sharp.

The audience gasped.

Esther sat frozen. Her hand trembled. Her body had gone rigid. Someone near her muttered a prayer under their breath. Others held still, waiting to see what would happen next.

Tania stood, expression unreadable.

A small, tight smirk at her lips. She turned. Returned to center stage. Bowed once.

Silence.

She left without applause. She didn't want it.

Esther could win the cash prize. Take home the trophy.

Tania didn't need those. Esther's silence was prize enough.

Chapter Thirty-Four

Leslie was the first to tell him. In bed, or what the movies got right: pillow talk. Walker knew because he'd written those scenes for Jack Warner, provided the couple slept in separate beds like an episode of *I Love Lucy*.

Half-awake, he heard it.

The ceiling fan rattled faintly above them. Rome's humidity made everything feel damp.

"The coup failed."

"What time is it?" He heard the words, but his body needed orientation.

"Time is the arrow we need to change in midflight."

His hands washed over his face. "Too early for philosophy, Les. How did you find out?"

She didn't answer that. She said, "Meersby will need to be talked down from the ledge."

"Find out from Miles?"

Made sense. Meersby had a direct line to Darbyshire in the field.

"Not Miles. Dulles."

He looked. She said, "He called. You were asleep. I answered."

"That must've scandalized him."

"Nothing dulls snakeskin."

Walker pointed to the ceiling. "They might be listening."

"The least of your problems. You should reconsider whether you're cut out for this."

He sat up. "Where's this coming from? What prompted that?"

"It's not your fault."

"I don't have the details."

"Doesn't matter."

"I was waiting on Bernays to do his part."

"Still doesn't matter."

He threw the sheet aside. The fan kept rattling. Rome's heat was already creeping in through the shutters.

"I get it. I'm the lead. No excuses. Dulles say anything else?"

"Kim is babysitting two Xerox machines, thanks to Jack and Sheldon, and the Shah fled."

"Fled where and with whom or what?" He sat on the edge of the bed. He heard Leslie dressing—a zipper pulled, the soft thud of shoes on carpet. His thoughts turned to improvisation. Be agile.

"Shah went to Baghdad. Wife and sister in tow. Might've taken the housekeys."

His mind woke up. "So he's exiled himself until recalled."

"No."

He turned. "What do you mean, no?"

"He's en route to Rome."

"Rome? He's coming here?"

Leslie searched her clutch. Contents rustled in her hands. "To the Excelsior."

Walker blinked. "Dulles know?"

"That's a stupid question. Of course, he knows. He arranged it."

"How do you sneak a foreign dignitary into a foreign country without the press or the Pope knowing?"

He stood and stretched. His joints cracked. The stiffness was part heat, part tension.

"Speaking of matters Catholic, how is Clare?"

Leslie crossed the room, her heels tapping out a rhythm across the floor.

"Dulles can make anything happen, Walker. The how isn't important. What you do next is. As for Clare, the doctor has her on fluid therapy. Investigators traced the cause to the wallpaper and paint in her room."

"You mean arsenic, and what investigators?"

She nodded. "My guess, Andreotti's men. Dulles asked for you. Get dressed."

He rubbed his temples. The late-summer heat pressed in like a heavy blanket.

"You're not my secretary. I know."

"And I'm not your nursemaid either. But you need to be sharp for this."

His mind flickered to the *pensione*. To Andreotti.

"What was with that earlier crack? That I should reconsider?"

She hesitated. Then: "You sleep too well for a case officer."

"I know this was all a test."

Leslie stopped, seemed surprised. "What test?"

"Something I was told. Never mind. Where are you going?"

"Meersby, remember?"

"Right, the man and his ledge. You have to give him two lumps of sugar instead of one. Kim stomps his foot, and the British make that face like they've sucked a lemon."

Leslie stiffened. "You don't seem to find me so Victorian in bed."

He bowed slightly. "And for that I'm grateful."

She shook her head. Her earrings caught the morning light, gold arcs swinging as she moved.

"My job is to keep MI6 on the rails. And about that earlier dig. What I meant is you sleep too long and too deep. You won't have that luxury once the job's yours. Not if you want to keep it."

She moved for the door. "And on that note, I'm off before Meersby gives Dulles the Churchill salute—and the V won't be for Victory."

* * *

Walker stood there like he was in the army again. At attention. This time, it was Allen Dulles instead of Jack Marshall. A luxury office instead of a field tent. He was to be debriefed.

"The coup failed, but this is not over," Dulles said. "I can count on Kim being Kim. Darbyshire will regroup and reassess, whereas Kim will charge ahead. It's one of the rare times you count on the bull's instinct to charge. Let the British have their cup of tea before they tally-ho and rally. Thoughts, Walker?"

"The propaganda, Bernays's work, sir."

"Edward was slow to assemble the materials, but he did. It's not your fault."

"Doesn't matter." Walker thought of Leslie. Responsibility fell on the officer in charge.

"Don't be so hard on yourself, Walker." A rare smile from Dulles. "Edward Bernays is a perfectionist, and while I admire that, it can be a liability—in the arts and in life. You know that. You're a writer. If you worried about every damn word, nothing would get on the page. Don't you agree?"

Walker met his gaze. "While I appreciate the leniency, sir, this isn't a screenplay."

Dulles looked at him a beat longer than necessary. "Don't be so sure about that. Don't forget, we're in the business of scenes and believable illusions."

The office smelled of polished wood and citrus, of something Mediterranean. Walker stood still, listening to philosophy from the cobra dressed as a professor in the full swelter of Rome in August.

"The people didn't rise?" he asked.

"They rose. Kim and Norman made sure of that. It's the generals who didn't rally. Mosaddegh got wind of it. His man shut it down at the palace."

"The stone in Kim's shoe?"

"Correct. Bahram Saidi has proved himself to be an impediment to our success. Mosaddegh is our lion in the desert—cagey and wise enough to have replaced Afshartous with Saidi. I thought him hobbled once Afshartous was out of the way. I was wrong."

That had to sting. Walker waited, kept at attention. Dulles delivered.

"Contingencies are simple. Let Kim man the Xerox machines, and Darbyshire will ask Zahedi to mobilize the men under his command. No coup succeeds without the military."

Walker didn't know if the Director sought agreement or simply stated fact.

Walker asked, "And Darbyshire can convince Zahedi?"

Dulles answered. "Promise a position, and money does the rest."

"Darbyshire has the money."

"Seven hundred thousand pounds."

Walker took that in. Let the British think they controlled the purse strings.

"Not that it seems to matter now that Kim has the diplomatic pouch. Did Darbyshire see the materials from Bernays?"

"It matters." Dulles's expression cooled. "He resented the fact that he didn't write the Farsi himself. A clean blow to his ego. Time is of the essence. Norman Darbyshire knows the tightrope is taut, and one wrong move, the juggler is dead."

Walker, the writer, appreciated the analogy. He almost smiled but didn't.

"And Kim's ego, since he's the delivery boy?"

"Kim is fluent in Arabic. I counted on him not knowing a lick of Farsi. He looked at the material from Bernays like a child, searching for pictures. Kim isn't one for crossword puzzles, Walker, but he's good at sharpening pencils and wearing down erasers. His Arabic will be useful when I assign him to Egypt."

"Egypt." The word caught. Walker suppressed disbelief.

"Suez. But that's a story for another day. Tux up, Walker."

"Tux up?"

Dulles looked at him like he'd answered a geometry question with finger paint. "Tuxedo. You and Leslie will join me tonight. Dinner with the Shah and his sister."

Walker nodded. "And his wife? I heard she came with him."

Dulles picked up a sheet of paper. A cue and a signal. He was nearly done with him.

"She did. But Empress Soraya took ill. Stress. I have Clare's doctor on her. She'll recover with rest. It's the Shah's sister, Princess Ashraf, you need to keep your eye on. Formidable. And the true Shah."

Walker let a second pass. "And Clare?"

"Still on the mend."

To Walker, this all dropped like a coin into water.

Walker had read about it, researching one of those potboilers for Warner.

Arsenic in wallpapers. Dresses. Book covers. Infants died in nurseries where steam heat turned the pigment into vapor. Women wasted away as poison crept through their skin. Readers met stories that could kill. The tell was always green. Scheele's Green.

"Andreotti's men found the source?" Walker asked.

"Wallpaper. That was old. Already there. The paint was new—and not."

"KGB?"

"You're not Simple Simon. You know the answer." Dulles didn't look up. "See you at dinner."

* * *

The Excelsior was the man's HQ, so Dulles made all the arrangements for the Shah. Citizens of Rome did not know about the royal entourage. The KGB did, no doubt, and the Vatican—the world's oldest sanctuary of secrets. Andreotti would know.

The private dining room was secured. Walker decided against the white dinner jacket. He chose a jacket in midnight blue, trousers with a silk side stripe, black patent leather shoes, cufflinks with French cuffs, and a bowtie. Leslie, while dressing, approved. She didn't have to help like a mother or sister would.

She'd chosen an elegant evening gown. Floor-length, deep navy to his midnight blue. Her hair up like Deborah Kerr. Earrings simple, enough to catch the light, but not enough to upstage Princess Ashraf. The dress moved like water when she walked.

They walked into a room dimly lit by chandeliers, with an unobstructed view of the quiet Roman streets outside. The room was air-conditioned, which added to the cool and cold personalities in the room. The windows, heavy with drapery, blurred the sound of Vespas and late summer voices. Heat pressed against the panes, but inside, the temperature belonged to another season, one colder and calculated.

Dulles sat at the head, his expression one of quiet control. Leslie, watchful, sat opposite, her posture impeccable, her eyes calculating, aware of everything in the room and its occupants. Walker was off to one side, a bit relaxed, though still on edge. He caught a glimpse of his own reflection in the silverware—composed on the surface, but his pulse ticked like a telegram.

The Shah maintained his dignity as a guest and not the host. His twin sister, Princess Ashraf, sat beside him, gaze sharp. Like Leslie, she assessed everyone in the room.

Princess Ashraf was the true power behind the throne, the steel spine her brother lacked. Wearing Persian couture, hair set and coiffed, makeup elegant but not overdone. She was a woman aware that she was being watched. She wore her signature gem, a pin with a pink diamond. Not gaudy. Elegant—and her scepter.

Dulles initiated the pleasantries.

"Your Majesty, I trust your journey here was without incident?"

"The flight from Baghdad, or the failure at home?"

Dulles didn't let it get under his skin. "Failure is a strong word. Unfortunate misstep, yes. But not the end."

Ashraf's voice cut through, no mistaking her sharp intelligence or disappointment.

"Temporary setbacks have a way of turning into permanent ones. Rome used to exile their trouble, not become a destination for trouble."

There was a lull. Silence. Everyone recognized the pointed nature of Ashraf's remark. Leslie tilted her head slightly, her eyes locked with Ashraf's for a fraction of a second.

"Wish to say something, dear?"

"I'm a woman. I don't think the men here would like to hear my opinion."

"It must be hard to imagine how we manage our daily lives when they write our history for us. Please speak freely, dear. I'll listen to them, but I'll hear you."

"Men may write history, but women know the price of victory is patience and... secrets."

Ashraf raised her glass, nodded, and smiled at Leslie. Walker watched the gesture, gracious on the surface, but it carried the weight of a verdict.

Dulles leaned forward, thankful for the lead that Leslie had created.

"Diplomacy has its place. We must all be clear-eyed about what needs to happen next."

The princess held her wineglass by the stem and turned it. "Saidi and General Zahedi."

They proceeded through the courses. The Shah complimented the wine, an Italian vintage was a change of pace from his usual shiraz. He interjected some lines from the poet Hafez.

His sister was playful but pointed. "His thoughts are on the wine and the meal, while his country and our fate hang in the balance."

The Shah found a vertebrate. "I didn't forget that the peacock represents our lineage. People think pride and vanity, but forget that the bird is known to scream."

Ashraf lifted an eyebrow, not amused. "You've found your voice, then. Let's hope you keep it when it matters."

"I listened to Leslie. The word that my ears heard loudest was patience."

"We must act before they devour us, brother."

As the meal wound down, Dulles rose first. His body language conveyed a sense of finality to the evening's discussions. The Shah, his face unreadable, his gaze sharp.

Dulles held up the after-dinner drink. He looked not at the Shah, but at Ashraf. "This time, we get it right."

Chapter Thirty-Five

Unlike the room used the night before or Dulles' own office, this was smaller, a suite once a reading room for special guests, now converted into a Situation Room. The ceiling was lower, the air thicker, despite the faint hum of fans. The room smelled faintly of cordite and damp paper from the constant shuffling of telegrams, cable briefs, and tear sheets from the telex machine in the corner.

Heavy velvet drapes were drawn tight across the windows, blocking the sunlight. It reminded Walker of a war bunker, the same atmosphere as Hitler's final days beneath Berlin.

On the walls, a pinned map of Tehran. Thumbtacks—what Leslie said the British called drawing pins—identified military barracks, key city squares, newspaper offices, and radio stations.

In the room with Dulles were the Shah, his sister, Leslie, and Walker.

A single telephone sat at the edge of the table, but most messages came by encrypted cable, on teletype paper, or were delivered via couriers from the U.S. embassy.

A courier delivered a pouch and left. Dulles unsealed it. There was a single piece of paper, and a newspaper. He didn't read to himself. He read aloud.

"Tehran reports Saidi was seen entering the Interior Ministry building with Afshartous's former adjutant. Crowd growing outside. Radio Tehran has issued a new editorial that is pro-Mosaddegh. No sign of Zahedi."

Princess Ashraf shook her head. "Afshartous taunts us from the grave."

"If Zahedi doesn't come out of hiding soon, we're not just losing this coup," Leslie said. "We're handing Iran to the Tudeh."

"A loss of oil, a victory for the Communists," Dulles answered. The voice, clinical.

Walker spoke. "And if Zahedi emerges unarmed? That's suicide."

Known for her outspokenness and pragmatism, Ashraf said what nobody else would:

"Who is responsible for Saidi?"

Without hesitation, Dulles answered, "That's Walker's decision to make."

Ashraf focused her eyes on Walker, now that she had an answer.

"I suggest you decide, sooner than later. Time is momentum. Saidi will muster support for his campaign and revenge for Afshartous. He remembers his closest friend."

"I understand that he remembers his mentor," Walker said.

"Understand this," Ashraf said, and paused. "What Saidi remembers most is not how Afshartous died. It's that the man had been tortured and strangled. The gunshot was mercy."

Busy with other papers, Dulles said, "Walker is known to be decisive. He makes decisions so others don't have to."

Ashraf seemed to accept what Dulles said. "Ex parte. Excellent. I was worried because he seems the quiet type."

Leslie, glass down after a sip of water. "Women know it's the quiet ones who merit attention—or caution."

"I'll take your word for it. Otherwise, every time you see Saidi's name in the papers, think about Soviet troops crossing oil fields."

Walker stood to give his legs circulation. His chair scraped loudly against the marble floor. He stepped out for some fresh air, not amused to have been called the quiet type by a woman who sat beside her brother, who hadn't said one word.

Not one.

The Shah hadn't spoken, but he had listened. His fingers toyed with a letter opener on the table, an idle gesture, or perhaps a private pressure valve. When Walker left, he followed the motion with his eyes, then returned to tracing the curve of the blade with his thumb.

* * *

Later in the day, a cable arrived. Roosevelt, in Tehran, reported momentum. Xerox machines hot from print runs, hired muscle to distribute them, and cause mayhem. He had money on the streets for both, and for luring the undecided among the military.

The meat of the message, however, was one line:

SAIDI = CRITICAL. EXPECT DECISION.

Dulles read it without comment, then slowly folded it.

He'd wait for Walker's return so he could pass it on to him.

* * *

After a brief recess, they reconvened in the room. The air smelled of coffee and cheap glue from all of the ink from Telex sheets. The Shah was near the window. Leslie was speaking to him in French, the language of diplomacy. He seemed calmer—a good thing—but still uncertain, as expected. His sister was the anchor to his boat and their throne.

Later, Leslie drifted toward Dulles at the desk. No end to paperwork.

He looked to the Shah, then to her. "How is he?"

"Better spirits. His wife's doctor gave him a good report."

"One less worry," Dulles said, and returned his attention to his papers.

Leslie looked to Walker, who appreciated the setup. Dulles sat between them. She was the angel, and he was the devil.

She motioned for a word near the window.

"I understand now," she said to Walker.

"What's that?"

"The test is Saidi."

Dulles stopped reading, looked over his shoulder at Walker. "Decision?"

"Cable Kim. Code Delta-Echo-Alpha-Delta."

Chapter Thirty-Six

ulles allowed none of the hotel's staff into the Situation Room. The Persian carpet looked worn thin from relentless pacing, and the mahogany table gleamed beneath layers of dispatches and cigarette ash. The windows remained shuttered, the air stale, a faint sourness of sweat and cold tobacco clinging to the drapes, though Dulles had lifted the sash to let in the unexpected chill of morning. The heavy curtains muffled the outside world, filtering the light into a dim, bruised amber.

The large map of Iran mounted on the wall was now cluttered with red and black strings, pins stretched from Abadan to Qazvin, but all threads returned to Tehran.

There was no food on the table. Only ashtrays, whiskey glasses, and the stale odor of cigarettes. Ashraf chain-smoked. Discriminate and decisive in all matters, her nicotine was her one indulgence: she smoked whatever was offered and had exhausted the Homas she'd brought from Iran. Though Dulles favored pipe tobacco, he'd secured cartons of Camels for her, a silent diplomatic gesture.

An aide knocked and waited at the door. He handed Leslie a single envelope. She read it silently, then passed it to Dulles.

FLASH MESSAGE – ROOSEVELT, TEHRAN
SAIDI NEUTRALIZED. BAZAAR IN MOTION. CROWDS IN SOUTH MARKET. ROYALIST FLIERS REAPPEARING. RADIO TEHRAN SIGNAL UNSTABLE. MOMENTUM BUILDING.

Dulles read, then folded the note slowly. "Saidi is dead. Roosevelt says the tide is turning."

Ashraf let out a long plume of gray smoke. "Death brings life back to the streets."

Leslie said nothing, but glanced at Walker.

He didn't look at her. He disliked himself, hated the smoke more.

No one asked for details. Dulles, almost gentle, said, "It was necessary."

The silence was short-lived. The teletype machine resumed its low, percussive chatter like a typewriter receiving orders from the void.

Something else was coming through.

* * *

After lunch, Dulles returned, a piece of paper in his hand.

The silent Shah spoke for the first time all day. "Good news?"

Dulles nodded. "Radio Tehran was silent for ninety minutes. Bazaar merchants have closed shops to show solidarity with Zahedi. An army unit in District Seven flew the royal flag." He pushed a new pin into the map. "All well and good, but no sign of Mosaddegh."

He stepped back for a fresh look at the map.

"The Shah's name is in the air. Tehran remembers who wears the crown."

Walker approached, asked to see the paper in his hand. Dulles passed it to him.

"Nice wave of momentum we've built. But I've done my share of surfing in Malibu. Balance is necessary to avoid a wipeout."

Ashraf extinguished her cigarette. "Your point is taken, Walker. But you're on the wave, not chasing it. My advice is ride it. And ride it hard."

Walker found Leslie across the room, absently pulling the chain around her neck up to her lips. She chewed it, gently. A quiet tell. He'd never seen her nervous until now.

* * *

Alone outside, Walker and Leslie shared a moment. She'd 'borrowed' a cigarette from the princess. He watched her light it, take the first draw.

"You smoke now."

"It's impolite to point out vices."

"Sorry."

"Sorry about the decision?"

"You heard Allen. It had to be done."

She looked at him, blew the smoke away from his face.

"We've both killed, up close. You'd think a shot from a distance would make it easier, but it doesn't, does it?"

"Death is death, Leslie. Generals do it. Presidents do it. One is trained for it. The other learns to live with it."

She made a face at the cigarette. "That's fucking harsh."

"The decision, or the cigarette?"

Her heel crushed the stub. "Widower with three kids. Did you know that?"

"I know."

Chapter Thirty-Seven

Dulles recognized the change in mood and tempo and chose another room to honor it. While the rest slept, Dulles arranged for the map, the telex, and other items to be relocated to one of the Excelsior's salons, a grand room once meant for Brahms and Berg, now conscripted for empire.

The Situation Room was now the Nerve Center.

High ceilings, heavy paneling, and gold-leaf mirrors line the walls, but the room remains dark, secretive, its hush like velvet. When they arrived, it was ready with strong coffee. A glass ashtray glistened in the light, prepared for Ashraf's cigarettes.

An invigorated Shah strode in, seeing Dulles, who never seemed to sleep. "Any news on Zahedi?"

"He's taken the radio station first, then the Interior Ministry."

"Excellent," the voice came from Ashraf. "Blood is in the veins."

"Like to keep it there, and off the walls and sidewalk," Walker said.

"The world is awake and watching. In seventy-two hours, brother, the crown is on your head."

Leslie cleared her throat. "It's usually men who are premature." She flinched a smile at the innuendo. "Lest we forget, Mosaddegh is afoot, or more accurately, on foot."

Dulles looked up. "Leslie is right. We shouldn't rush the conclusion because it feels good to say it."

"Any word from Kim?" Walker asked.

"Zahedi ready to act at dawn. Royalist generals meet tonight. They maneuver at midnight. Awaiting green light, but here we are at Zahedi's elbow. Kim can't reach him. It's not your call to make. We have no choice but count on him."

"Sit and wait then? The theme song to my life," Walker said.

Dulles appreciated the humor. "I don't like dependencies any more than you do, Walker, but if Zahedi screws up, the next bit of news we hear is him against the wall, no blindfold. If he's lucky to make it that far, he might earn himself a cigarette."

Ashraf added, "And the firing squad lights it for him."

* * *

Mid-morning, they sat on the sofa. The radio sputtered, a fog of static, but a clear signal cut through.

"Zahedi has appeared at the Army Headquarters. Loyalists seen near Baharestan Square."

Leslie sat forward. "He's shown his face. Think he's played his hand too early."

Dulles' hand came up. "Wait and see. Listen."

"Thought he'd lie low until this evening."

Dulles shushed her.

"Crowds in Sepah Square. Tudeh banners torn down. Rumors of Mosaddegh fleeing. People chant the Shah's name. Pahlavi. Pahlavi."

"It's begun," Ashraf said.

Walker stepped up to the map, moved a red pin to mark Zahedi's emergence.

"Now we have to hold the frame. If Radio Tehran flips, the country follows."

An hour later, several cigarettes in the ashtray, a cable arrived from Kim.

RADIO TEHRAN BREACHED. ZAHEDI FORCES INSIDE. MOSADDEGH COMPOUND OVERRUN. TROOPS DEFECT- ING. CROWDS FLOODING STREETS. IT'S DONE. REPEAT: IT'S OURS.

An expressionless Dulles. "That's the sound of the empire salvaged."

A satisfied Ashraf. "It was always ours. The question was when."

Walker sank into the cushion, exhaling for the first time in what felt like days.

The realization hadn't registered with the Shah. "They want me back home?"

There was something cracked to the words—relief, disbelief, maybe fear.

Dulles. "They'll welcome you with flowers. And with fear."

Leslie added the twist. "Fear works. Today, at least."

Chapter Thirty-Eight

With success assured, Dulles shifted operations from the Excelsior to the U.S. Embassy, now that the press was abuzz with the news from Tehran. The embassy drawing room, a classical Roman space with Baroque flourishes, felt ornate compared to their Situation and Nerve rooms at the hotel. The air was chilled from the air conditioning, the smell of leather chairs, floor wax, and crisp paper.

Congratulatory cables had been arranged in stacks for the Shah. Some in French, others in English, a few in Farsi. Some were from monarchist factions, others from unnamed 'friends of the throne.' The Shah sat at a large writing desk, reviewing them like a man leafing through condolences at a wake. The days and restless nights had left him tired, almost timid, as if he had shrunk from the stress. He'd been short with his wife, but now he had empathy for her. She had wilted when they first landed in Baghdad, relieved later in Rome, safe but exhausted.

Ashraf, by contrast, seemed rejuvenated, as if she already had ideas, and it wasn't on how she'd decorate the court upon return. Dulles seemed ageless, immune to bad weather or news. Leslie, true to her heritage, maintained the British upper lip. Vigilant, mindful of the human cost. Fresh suit, composed posture, but eyes that betrayed the toll of command, standing apart, quiet and haunted, was Walker.

The Shah opened a cable, read it aloud.

"Commander Farhadi sends his allegiance. Royal Guard unit secured the entrance to the Foreign Ministry building. Zahedi has assumed provisional authority."

He put it down. No smile.

"It seems they welcome me again."

Ashraf patted his shoulder. "They always did. They only needed to miss you."

Dulles stepped forward. "The British ambassador is preparing a formal message. Your return is in doubt—his statement is a matter of protocol."

The Shah looked to Dulles. "And the Americans?"

"You'll find that silence is worth more than speeches."

Leslie walked over, placed another envelope down. "From Baghdad. King Faisal's court is arranging safe passage. You'll have a full escort when you depart."

Walker: "We'll see to it that you get to Ciampino, safe and sound."

The Shah nodded.

In the small inner courtyard of the embassy, Walker and Leslie stepped outside. The air smelled of rosemary and diesel from the embassy motor pool.

Walker was quiet. He thought Leslie would speak first. She didn't. He did.

"This is what history feels like. They cheered in the streets."

"Some did. The rest stood back and watched."

"Not enough for you, is that it?"

"History simply needs a good camera angle after it's written."

They stood in silence for a moment. Long enough to notice an unexpected breeze.

"Do you think they'll let him rule?"

"The Company will let him wear the crown. Rule? My money is on his sister."

"Mine is on Dulles."

* * *

In the afternoon, they met back at the Excelsior for a brief discussion of logistics.

Dulles informed the Shah and Ashraf that a small plane would take them to Baghdad, then onward to Tehran. Roosevelt would meet them on the tarmac.

"And the crowds?" the Shah asked.

"They'll be there, Your Majesty. Our leaflets will make sure of that. You'll hear chanting before the wheels touch ground."

"And if they don't chant?"

Ashraf pulled at her brother's arm. "They will."

Dulles added, "And if they don't, we'll say they did."

Chapter Thirty-Nine

The sun rose over the outskirts of Rome.

Ciampino Airport, once a military airfield and now a modest hybrid hub for civilian and military flights, hummed with morning activity. The tarmac glinted with dew, and in the hazy orange light, a sleek silver aircraft awaited, its stairs lowered, engines idling, waiting to carry the Shah, his wife, and sister back into power.

A small escort of embassy cars pulled up near the plane. No journalists, no press, only men in dark suits, sunglasses on, and a handful of Italian military staff for security. The departure was deliberately low-profile, coordinated through embassy back channels and intermediaries.

The Shah, dressed in full military regalia, shoulders square, looked paler than he felt, but determined to play his part. Ashraf appeared regal, calm, electric with certainty.

Queen Soraya sat in the car, visibly tired. She did not step onto the tarmac until the last moment, when she accepted a small bouquet of roses from Dulles and his regrets that they had not had more time together. He hoped she felt better. She thanked him for the doctor and for all that he had done, "of which I have no idea," she said.

Walker stood off to the side. Leslie was not there.

A light breeze caught the hem of the Shah's coat. His hands trembled slightly, but his face held.

"It's a cliché in American cinema, Mr. Dulles, but thank you for everything."

"Your Majesty. It has been an honor."

"You have restored more than a crown, Mr. Dulles."

"We've restored a symbol. The crown you'll have to earn back."

Ashraf answered: "He will. He will, Mr. Dulles. Thank you." She glanced to the side.

"Please say goodbye to Leslie for me. It's nice to see a strong woman in person, and not just on the stage."

A small military band played a nondescript melody.

The Shah ascended the stairs, Ashraf behind him. At the top, he turned and saluted.

It was for a photograph no one was there to take.

Soraya, pale and dignified, was helped up last. Like Lot, she did not look back.

The door closed. The stairs were wheeled away.

The plane began to taxi.

As the jet lifted off over the rooftops of Rome, the black smoke behind it vanished into the sky.

Dulles watched and, without looking at Walker, said:

"Good job."

"I wasn't expecting that—from you of all people."

"Likely the only time you'll ever hear it from anyone. Where we live, nobody thanks us."

Walker thought of ghosts.

* * *

Later, at the hotel, in their room, Walker sat on the bed, his legs over the edge, his tie undone. Leslie stood by the window, eyes on Rome but not seeing its glorious past.

"Think he's ready for what's waiting?"

"You're the one who told me it doesn't matter."

"What's that supposed to mean?"

"He's not going back for them. He's going back because we said he could.

Chapter Forty

His sleep was terrible. Walker awakened to a sound in the room. He looked to his left. She wasn't there.

That noise again. He rubbed his eyes and lifted his head. She sat in the chair near the desk. She peered over the edge of the latest edition of *Il Tempo*, a morning daily with a strong anticommunist slant. The pages ruffled.

"*Buongiorno*. Not sleep well?"

"Not great. Wish I could've slept longer, though."

"You might be Case Officer material after all."

Wearing a see-through camisole, she set aside the paper and rose from her chair. She walked over to the bed. He was under a light bedsheet. She didn't tug at him, just ran her hand down the length of it, soothing out the material.

"Saidi bothers you. As it should. But this is the life we lead. Decisions made, consequences compartmentalized, burden carried." Her hand moved. "Time to get up."

He hated that phrase. It sounded like something from the farm, or worse, 'up and at 'em'—the words the sergeants would bark out to their men in the trenches of World War I before they went over the top into machine-gun fire.

"I don't want to get up."

Leslie stood, and for a second he thought she might yank the sheet off him.

"Think someone's already up," she said.

She peeled off her nightwear, the sheet over him, and mounted him.

"I call this field conditioning," she said.

"You're not wrong."

"Call it what you want. My advice is *carpe diem.*"

She established a slow and certain rhythm. He looked up at her. His hands enjoyed her hips, his hands on her waist.

She rested her hands on his chest. "Focus on the moment," she said. "But always keep your eyes on the mission."

He stared at her. She felt good. The name Dulles did not.

"Emotions don't last," she whispered.

He knew what the next moan meant.

* * *

They strolled down Via Veneto in search of caffeine. Plane trees shaded the wide boulevard. Her polished shoes clicked against the warm cobblestones. Vespas buzzed past like impatient bees, riders in crisp shirts and dark sunglasses. The scent of gasoline hung in the air. So did the smell of ground coffee from cafés, where white-jacketed waiters coaxed tourists inside.

One spotted them. *"Due caffè, subito!"*

They sat at a thumbtack called a table, which made Walker think of the maps in Dulles' rooms. Porcelain clinked. Steam hissed. The heat already built in the street.

Women in full skirts and silk scarves chattered—Italian sounded melodic no matter the subject. Tourists nearby, a wife wanted to see the Spanish Steps, or the apartment where Keats had died. Her husband wanted to see the Colosseum.

Their waiter delivered two espressos.

Across from Walker, a lone traveler—not American—read Graham Greene.

"Miss it?" Leslie asked, cocking her head and watching him closely.

"Miss what?" Walker replied, eyes on the crema in his espresso.

"Writing. You're living the adventure, but part of you wants to be behind the typewriter."

"Is that a sin?" He lifted the cup, taking a slow, deliberate sip.

"I don't believe in sin. Or heaven. Or hell. No old man in the sky with a beard. No one downstairs with a tail and a pitchfork." Leslie shrugged.

He sipped again. The espresso hit hard. His eyes glanced toward the street. "When you said 'old man,' I thought you meant Dulles."

"He picked you because you're a writer." Leslie's voice softened, almost a tease.

"When we met, he mentioned a few. Greene was one of them." Walker leaned back, finger tapping the rim of his cup.

"Charming man. Serial philanderer. MI6. But who am I to judge?" Leslie said, her tone half-amused, half-serious.

"Brunch is with Dulles and Clare. What should I expect?" Walker asked, eyebrows raised.

"Perfunctory congratulations. Then assessment. Clare's coming late on purpose." Leslie glanced down at her cup, fingers curling around the handle.

"A hot wash then?" Walker pushed, voice low.

"What's a hot wash?" Leslie asked.

He explained how he and Jack and the boys would sit around after a mission, honest about what went wrong, what worked. No rank. Just facts and discussion. Leslie listened, her eyes digesting.

"Sounds so democratic, but Dulles doesn't believe in democracy. Only outcomes. The only things he considers democratic are hospitals and death." Leslie's voice was dry.

"Why?" Walker's gaze sharpened.

"Because everyone ends up horizontal." She shrugged, a wry smile.

"And Clare?" Walker asked, leaning forward.

"Dulles gave her a different arrival time. She won't hear the full conversation." Leslie's tone dropped, an edge of caution creeping in.

"Deniability." Walker nodded slowly.

"Same reason she couldn't be in the war room." Leslie glanced around briefly, as if she suspected eavesdroppers.

"I doubt she faked arsenic poisoning." Walker's voice was skeptical.

"She could've claimed a Roman stomach. Said it was something she ate." Leslie shrugged again.

"But she didn't." Leslie pushed the cup away. A ring of crema coated the empty cup. Her fingers lingered on the table.

"About that arsenic…" Walker began.

"I know. Wallpaper. The paint." Leslie met his gaze steadily.

"You knew?" He frowned.

"Meersby told me." Leslie's voice was firm.

Walker shook his head, finished the last of his espresso. The bitterness seemed to settle over him.

"Back channels?" Walker asked, suspicion in his voice.

"Professional courtesy." Leslie's eyes narrowed slightly.

"Speaking of Meersby, how did Kim go over with Norman?"

"Like a lead balloon. Different egos, but same orbit." Leslie rolled her eyes. "Kim'll take credit, since he delivered the money, and he guarded those Xeroxes like a child guarding his toys."

"And Norman?"

"Took it. Didn't like it. Stiff upper lip." Leslie smirked.

"Lay back and think of England isn't just for women?"

"Exactly." That came with a smile.

"Like this morning?" Walker's voice was teasing.

"I didn't hear any complaints." Leslie took a napkin and dabbed her mouth. "Meersby told me something else. I saw it in the paper this morning."

"Related to the operation?" Walker asked.

"Tangential, I suppose." Leslie's brow furrowed.

Walker frowned. "I don't follow."

"Two bodies pulled from the Tiber. Russians. They didn't drown." Leslie's voice was low, the weight of the news sinking in.

Chapter Forty-One

The sixth floor, a recent addition to the Excelsior, offered rooftop dining that was both elegant and exclusive. Dulles, a legend for formality, a man who dressed like a professor, was both enigmatic and strategic with his words. He didn't know how to say thank you. This brunch, with its panoramic view of Rome, was his version of saying: *Job well done.*

Leslie and Walker walked out to a Rome of pale blue sky, the Basilica of St. Peter's in the distance, scattered examples of Romanesque architecture in Trastevere, the green spread of the Villa Borghese below. A faint shimmer on the horizon hinted at another scorching day. The rooftop carried the scent of citrus and heat-baked stone. Far below, the sound of cars on the Via Veneto.

Dulles sat, waiting for them. The white tablecloth pressed tight under silverware.

He stood, shook hands with Walker, and did *i baci*, the brief touch of cheeks, the graze of the lips, because 'when in Rome.' He gestured to the two chairs and mentioned the third was for Clare Booth Luce, who would arrive in fifteen minutes or so. He relayed the excuse that she was busy with official business, which they all knew was a lie.

Dulles pulled out the chair for Leslie. She sat. Walker took his chair last.

The chairs softly scraped the ground.

He wanted them alone, to debrief them before she joined them.

The tall bottle of mineral water made Walker think of his meeting with Andreotti.

A small silver tray of fresh *cornetti*, Italian croissants, was there, a small offering of figs, cherries, and melon to hold them over until Clare made her appearance. Two small porcelain cups of espresso steamed lightly in front of them. A third sat untouched.

Seated, his hand on the rim of his espresso cup that he was drinking, Dulles didn't waste time. They would talk about the coup in cloaked terms.

"Ever notice how Rome pretends it never fell?"

Walker glanced at the skyline. "Doesn't look fallen from here."

"That's the appeal. Marble and myth. Ideal cover for decay."

He took a careful sip, then set the cup down with precision. No clink, no echo.

Leslie asked for the bottle. Walker offered to pour. She said she could do it herself.

She poured mineral water, the glass sweating in her hand.

"Some ruins are more stable than new regimes."

Dulles glanced but didn't smile. "A romantic thought. Dangerous in our business."

His eyes flicked toward Walker, not sharp, just measuring.

Walker stepped into the verbal fray. "The Shah's in. Mosaddegh is out. Zahedi stands guard."

"That remains to be seen."

He didn't raise his voice. He didn't need to.

This surprised Walker, but not Leslie. "Did I miss something?"

"The name Ayatollah Kashani has come up in conversation. I'm certain Leslie can fill you in."

Dulles smiled from behind his small cup of espresso. Walker didn't know if this was another chess move, a seed of doubt planted between them, or MI6 and the Company.

Either way, Dulles had moved the first pawn forward.

"Is Washington pleased?" Walker asked.

"For now. That's not the same as success." Dulles set the cup down precisely.

Leslie asked, "Suggesting there is work to be done, here in Rome."

"Italy is a long-term project."

"A thumbnail sketch?" Walker asked.

"Thinking of an extended stay?"

"I have a writing project waiting for me."

"A novel, I hope. Not memoir," Dulles said.

"Fiction is truth. Truth, fiction."

Dulles nodded. "You wrote good dialogue for Jack Warner."

Walker shrugged. "He paid well, and on time. The thumbnail, or a postcard, please."

Dulles glanced to Leslie. "She's the analyst. Ask her."

"But I asked you," Walker said, but stopped. Leslie had placed her hand on his forearm. He looked to her.

"Italy is a peninsula, a country with no natural resources: no coal, no iron, no oil or gas, but some limited farmland."

"And your point is?" Walker asked, disoriented, from Iran to this detailed synopsis about the other I: Italy.

Leslie continued. "The one resource Italians have — and always have had — is their ingenuity."

Dulles interjected. "She can tell you later what the word *furbo* means. Go on, Leslie."

"In addition to the threat of Communism in Western Europe, Mr. Dulles is concerned with the northern Italian companies that declined aid from the Marshall Plan."

"I wasn't aware anyone refused, Walker said. "They don't want to repay the loans? It's my understanding Marshall was generous and fair. Hell, we were kind to the Germans after all they did."

Leslie leaned forward. "They declined because they realized accepting the money and aid to rebuild would make them dependent on a foreign entity. Guess who?"

Walker looked from her to Dulles.

"We don't celebrate. We rotate the chessboard. The game is always in play. Always."

Walker turned his attention back to her. She said, *"Sempre."*

It hung in the air, not as a flourish, but as a fact.

* * *

Church bells rang ten across the Tiber. She wore a white summer dress, large sunglasses, and a silk scarf pinned loosely around her shoulders. Her gait, though not brisk, would never suggest she had survived arsenic poisoning. Dulles and Walker stood. Dulles was the first to greet her.

"You look well, Madam Ambassador."

"Flattery will take you far, Allen. Hello, Walker and Leslie."

Walker beat Dulles to pulling out her chair. A small victory.

"Thank you, darling. One positive of being almost poisoned is that it has done wonders for my appetite. Let's hope the chef isn't Giulia Tofana. Arsenic was her signature dish."

"You're in good spirits, Madam Ambassador," Leslie said.

"Please, let it be Clare. I've been resurrected, thanks to Allen's resources." She placed her hand over his. "A wonderful team of physicians from the U.S. Navy Hospital in Naples."

"And the Villa Taverna?" Walker asked.

"Couldn't catch me dead in the place until it's been stripped, refurbished, and I had a priest from the Vatican bless the residence himself." Leslie noticed that Clare's hand had not moved.

* * *

They ordered a silver champagne bucket with fresh orange juice and chilled prosecco for mimosas. A waiter delivered frittata, a light *insalata caprese*, small plates of *pane tostato*, blood orange segments, and ricotta with honey. He poured the first round of prosecco.

Dulles refrained from alcohol as he liked to maintain all his senses for conversation.

"How was your morning?" Dulles asked.

"The usual."

CHAPTER FORTY-ONE

Leslie, curious, asked. "The usual?"

"You would completely understand, darling. A male journalist with the IQ of a Q-tip attempted to steal my thunder like he was Ty Cobb, in hot, spikes up. I set him straight."

Walker loved her. "What did this idiot say?"

She imitated the man's patronizing tone. Dry as reeds. *"Ambassador Luce, tell us what it's like to be the exception in politics, and care to comment about the difficulties of being a woman in power?"*

Leslie couldn't help but grin, and even Clare had managed to dent Dulles' granite façade.

"Oh, I set him straight. I said to him, 'Successes, as in plural. You imply I'm the rare bird? Don't worry, darling. I'll fly with that and take the rare honor of keeping the rest of the flock in line. As for a woman in power, I don't mind being underestimated. The boys in the room are in for a nice surprise. Makes victory all the sweeter. Speaking of victory," she rose, glass of prosecco in hand. "A toast. Stand up, please. You all deserve it."

They did. Luce said, *"Complimenti e tanti successi!"*

It didn't go unnoticed, especially by Dulles, that Clare had clinked glasses first with Leslie, who responded with, *"Alla tua."*

Chapter Forty-Two

The mountains were beginning to change. Not much, not yet. The color of rust flirted with the edges of the leaves. The evenings were cooler now, the lake quieter, less laughter around the resort. A kind of hush had settled in, with the seasonal goodbyes thick in the air.

Sheldon adjusted the cuffs of his linen shirt while he waited near the long driveway for the valet to bring his car around. He had let Ben know when he and Tania were leaving so they could say their farewells—the girls especially. Tania stood beside him, arms crossed, staring out toward the lake.

"I hate this place," she said, which was not quite the truth.

"I know," Sheldon replied.

Ben Morris approached with Judith walking a few paces ahead of him. Ruth carried a bag with a crooked handle and something else in her other hand, but Tania couldn't see what. Ben looked leaner than when they'd met. He had lost some weight. The divorce papers were finalized. The permit had come through for his building at Bush Terminal.

"End of the season," Ben said. "No more arts and crafts. No more all-you-can-eat food."

Tania, seeing Judith, said, "No more Esther, either."

Judith muttered, "Thank God."

Ruth, always quiet, seemed sadder. She clutched a worn teddy bear, one ear nearly gone.

"Back next year?" Ben asked Sheldon.

"Maybe. All depends on Tania here. She's scouting colleges. Road trips add up."

"I understand. She's a gift. She can sing, and then some."

Tania wasn't one to do the dramatic teen sigh. She stood her ground.

Ben leaned closer, lowering his voice. "Can I tell you something?"

"Sure, what is it?"

"I read the strangest thing in the paper this morning. About Shay O'Brien."

"What about him?"

"He's gone. As in *gone-gone.*"

Sheldon raised his brows. "Really?"

"Disappeared. Walked out of his office last Tuesday. No one's seen him since." Ben studied him. "Don't you think that's one hell of a coincidence, Sheldon?"

"You have feelings for the guy, after all he put you through?" Sheldon placed a hand on Ben's shoulder. "It's New York. The guy made enemies."

"What are you saying? The mob?"

"Why not? Jersey. Philly. A little old lady in Canarsie."

Ben snorted. "You're right." He held Sheldon's gaze. "Convenient is all I'm saying."

Sheldon didn't blink. "Sometimes the trash takes itself out."

Behind them, Judith called out, "We should go, but we want to say goodbye to Tania."

"Who's 'we'?" Ben said.

"Me and Ruth."

"And Sheldon is what, chopped liver with schmaltz and *gribenes?*"

Ben shook hands with Sheldon, then hugged him. Two hearty pats on the back.

"I'll see you when I see you. Girls, say your goodbyes while I go find our jalopy. One last ride for the old girl — now that I can afford a new set of wheels."

Judith and Ruth turned to Sheldon.

He understood they wanted privacy. He walked a few paces away, lighting a cigarette.

Tania didn't have the words, but she remembered the last time she'd seen her mother and father before they had disappeared, thanks to Stalin. She stood there.

Ruth was the emotional one. Judith was strong for her.

Judith hugged Tania, kissed her on the cheek, and whispered, "No more Esther and Pomeranians, thanks to you."

"No more Pomeranians."

Then came Ruth. She held back tears.

"It's okay, Ruthie. You'll be alright."

"You gave me those sunglasses."

"Yes, I did."

"I want you to have this." She handed Tania her teddy bear, hugged her tight, and ran off.

Tania watched them leave, waved, then walked down the small hill to Sheldon.

"You okay?" he asked, once they were inside the car.

Windows open, wind stirring through the trees, the first hint of woodsmoke in the air.

Tania said, "Shay O'Brien."

Sheldon repeated, "Shay O'Brien."

Chapter Forty-Three

Malibu. The ocean was a constant hush outside, the kind that swallowed answers. Walker didn't move at first. He watched the sky turn a shade of gunmetal over the water, the way it always did when the sun failed to deliver a dramatic farewell.

The phone rang. He let it go three times before answering.

"Walker."

Jack's voice came through like gravel rolled in a coffee can. "You sitting down?"

"Am I supposed to be?"

"Wouldn't hurt."

Walker turned from the view. He sat in the leather chair, the phone cord drawn tight like an excitable dog on a leash.

"Sheldon pulled it off," Jack said.

"I figured as much. Xeroxes saved the day."

"Kim would have you believe it was him."

Walker glanced at the manuscript on his desk, still a work in progress. "Trade go smoothly?"

"Permit's through. Divorce expedited. Like the kids say, it went swell."

Walker said nothing. He waited.

"Took some work, but it all lined up."

Walker said, "I guess a judge was easy to reach. City Hall?"

Jack sighed. "A bureaucrat who kept a sharp pencil."

"Pencil get broken?"

Jack hesitated. "More like, pencil disappeared."

"You made that call?"

"Not me," Jack said.

"Sheldon."

"Nope."

"Oh," Walker said.

"It's the company we keep."

"Any liabilities?"

"None that I see," Jack said. "Order came from Room 3603, Rockefeller Center. Sheldon sold a story. The pencil-pusher had enemies. Our guy bought it. Everyone's happy. Rome?"

"To use your words, it went swell."

Jack chuckled. "I figured as much. The old man?"

"Relieved to know he's on our side, but I met his Italian twin."

"You don't say. I've been told we all have a carbon copy somewhere. Leslie?"

"She sends her regards."

Walker stared at the typewriter.

"It's not like she's far, Walker. She's in L.A., unless she's moved."

"She hasn't."

"You okay?"

"No."

"Okay."

The line went quiet. A click.

The ocean kept on.

He heard a seagull screech, thought of a peacock.

Chapter Forty-Four

Walker stood at the edge of the bluff above Malibu, where the land fell away into a slow, steady roar of surf and mist. The telegram from Foggy Bottom was still in his jacket pocket, unopened. Dulles never asked questions in cables. He issued coordinates or riddles, like the Delphic oracle.

Inside the house, the light on the table caught the grain of the wood. There was that kind of silence found in rooms left alone for too long. Everything was in its place, but none of it felt like home.

Next to the typewriter sat a folded note from her.

She had left it at the bedside for him in Rome.

Dear Walker,

We were never meant to be here. Not in this place. Not after everything.

I left earlier than planned. I'm sure that doesn't surprise you.

You know why I was there, and you know what I did. I wasn't lying to you, but I wasn't exactly with you either. I told myself you knew it would be this way. So—no apologies. Not for that.

We'll both keep moving. I'll make sure you never have to answer for the parts I didn't share. But I know you're better than that.

It's not always easy to walk away. Even when the game is over. But sometimes, the only way out is to keep walking.

You won't hear from me again. But you'll understand why.

Take care, Walker.

—Leslie

He read it once, then again. There was nothing left to say. She had her reasons. He folded the note, placed it beside the typewriter. He'd leave it there. Let it be a page you turned. No answers. Just the soft silence of things that had been.

Outside, the ocean stretched wide and indifferent. The last of the daylight flickered on the horizon, the kind of light that didn't promise anything.

Below, the coastal homes blinked faintly through the mist. He could see people, shadows, quiet lives untouched by cables, coups, or the sharp edge of empire.

The keys waited for him. Ribbon spooled. Pages blank.

He didn't know what he'd write next.

But it wouldn't be a lie.

Afterword

Eyes to Deceit is a work of fiction.

Operation Ajax, the 1953 coup in Iran, and its tangled aftermath, are painfully real.

In August of that year, a democratically elected government was overthrown in Tehran through a covert operation led by the CIA and Britain's MI6. The target was Prime Minister Mohammad Mossadegh. The rationale was Cold War orthodoxy: containment, oil, and influence—but the consequences spiraled far beyond Iran's borders.

Characters like Walker and Leslie are imagined, as are the betrayals and private tensions that unfold in the Catskills that summer. The Borscht Belt resort and internal espionage plot are fictional. But the backdrop—the realpolitik, the shadows—was not.

Allen Dulles, Kermit 'Kim' Roosevelt, and Norman Darbyshire were real men, operating in real rooms. Darbyshire, a key MI6 operative, remained in the shadows for decades. His suppressed testimony features prominently in *Coup 53*, a 2019 documentary that reshaped our understanding of how this coup was executed.

This novel also includes figures like Clare Boothe Luce and Giulio Andreotti—both historical, both emblematic of a moment when diplomacy, ambition, and propaganda were indivisible. Their inclusion isn't a historical claim, but a reminder: once power moves in secret, it rarely stops at the border.

A note on chronology: Clare Boothe Luce's arsenic poisoning, which in reality occurred in 1954, has been shifted earlier for dramatic purposes. At the time, the cause was believed to be environmental, but there was speculation of foul play. In this fictional telling, that speculation becomes part of the plot.

Operation Ajax lit a fuse. It burned through repression, reprisals, and disillusionment until it exploded in 1979 with the Iranian Revolution and Hostage Crisis. What was framed as a strategic triumph in 1953 would later be seen as one of the Cold War's most shortsighted miscalculations.

This wasn't the last domino to fall. It was the first.

Fiction can't fix history.

But it can remind us what it felt like.

Recommended reading and viewing:

- *Coup 53* (2019), dir. Taghi Amirani. A revelatory documentary that brings suppressed history to light.
- *All the Shah's Men* by Stephen Kinzer. A vivid account of the coup and its architects.
- *Legacy of Ashes* by Tim Weiner. A wide-lens view of the CIA and its legacy.
- *The Oil Kings* by Andrew Scott Cooper. A deeper dive into U.S.–Iranian relations through the Cold War.

Acknowledgments

I'm grateful to my publisher, Level Best Books, for their continued faith in my work. Thank you, Dames of Detection.

Hugs and friendship for Shawn Reilly Simmons, my editor.

I'm thankful for the generosity and feedback from my sensitivity reader Mally Becker, and continuity editor Deb Well. I'm grateful for the attentive eyes of my proofreader Tina de Bellegarde.

As always, nothing but gratitude to my fellow Level Best authors, and to friends of the pen and keyboard in crime fiction, the best and most supportive community around for a writer.

About the Author

Gabriel Valjan is a member of ITW, MWA, and a lifetime member of Sisters in Crime. He is the author of *The Company Files* and the *Shane Cleary Mysteries* with Level Best Books. His work has been nominated for the Agatha, Anthony, and the Silver Falchion awards. Gabriel received the 2021 Macavity Award for Best Short Story and the Shamus Award for Best Original PI Paperback Novel in 2024. He is a regular contributor to the blog *Criminal Minds* and an active supporter of writers on social media. Gabriel lives in Boston and answers to a tuxedo cat named Munchkin.

AUTHOR WEBSITE:

https://gabrielvaljan.com/

SOCIAL MEDIA HANDLES:

https://x.com/GValjan
https://www.instagram.com/gabrielvaljan/

Also by Gabriel Valjan

Shane Cleary Mystery Series
Liar's Dice
Hush Hush
Symphony Road
Dirty Old Town

Company Files Series
The Devil's Music
The Naming Game
The Good Man